THE MAID'S BLESSING

Victorian Romance

SADIE HOPE

Join my newsletter

INTRODUCTION

This is a romance set in the often dismal streets of Victorian London. I hope you will enjoy my stories as I share them with you. I have only just started sharing my writing and am still learning. I do appreciate you, my readers, for all the wonderful feedback I have received.

Some of you love the fact that I have serialised these books about Valeria, Allen, and Nora, others have not been so happy

INTRODUCTION

I decided to do it this way as you, my readers, were asking for stories and this way it was easier to get them out quickly.

Each book can be read alone, and has its own story, but if you wish to read them from the start they are:

The Orphan's Courage
    The Orphan's Hope
    The Mother's Secret
    The Maid's Blessing

Sadie Hope
    Follow me on:
    Facebook/AuthorSadieHope

Join my newsletter for new release announcements and special offers
http://eepurl.com/dOVZDb

1

The London docks were a hive of industry. It was too much for Nora as she stood in the shadow of *HMS Catherine the Great*. Her heart was breaking yet the place was all business. The movement and noise, all directed to some purpose she could not quite fathom, made her feel ill, or possibly that was the morning sickness.

Despite its considerable size, the *Catherine the Great* was dwarfed by the steamer on the opposite quay. It was also relatively slow-moving by comparison and would take a good two weeks to reach Copenhagen with all the stops included. The great hulk would steal William away within the hour and the thought of not seeing him tore the breath from her body and left her legs weak.

The boat was boarding now, the crew getting ready to cast off in time with the noon-day gun which would be firing soon. As a result, there was less bustle than there had been when everyone was still saying their good-byes and double checking that their loved ones had everything they would need for the voyage.

Nora searched the docks for William's sweet face but she could not find him amongst the people. The last few remaining passengers milled about beneath the towering boat, saying their goodbyes and farewells, reminding each other to dress warm and be careful of strangers.

The other steamer, across the quay, was taking on coal still and two huge cranes were moving British textiles aboard. It was crawling with men. The water between them was covered in the smoke from the tugs and small skiffs which puttered in and out of the shadows of the behemoths.

It felt like they were hemmed in by some vast and unfeeling animal, with all these mechanical organs working to some purpose she could only decipher by scientific study. That reminded her that she needed to remember to pass through Holborn on their way home to pick up supplies, for her anatomical analyses.

William had been too tied up with business concerns since their marriage and so Nora had taken over much of his work on prenatal development in the lower rungs of the animal kingdom. The study of the infants of other species made her increasingly aware of the body of her own child growing within her.

Allen touched her shoulder. "You all right, Nora? You look a little queasy."

He was right. She felt queasy, and not just because of the prospect of cutting into flesh. The morning sickness had been worse lately. She tried to hide it lest it worry William. She was sure it was worse because of her worry on account of this foolish trip.

Was it that obvious, she wondered? She did so want to put on a brave face for William. After all, he would not be gone long. A few weeks under power to Copenhagen. Then a few weeks of trading information with a range of Danish natural philosophers, librarians and historians. It would take him a few more weeks nailing down a deal with the Danish government for the plans for a more accurate chronometer he had developed. Then he would be on his way home, the journey back would be a few days on the *Catherine the Great* again. If it all went to schedule, he would be gone just only a few months. But it was their first time apart, and Nora had been racked by an eerie premonition. Seeing him leave took her back to her days in the orphanage. The days of despair and no hope. Without him she was nothing and the fear inside would not go away. A feeling had come upon her that this perfect life she now had couldn't last, but that was just foolish.

A flash of annoyance crossed her mind. What did he have to go all the way to Denmark for? Were there not plenty of business opportunities in Great Britain and its empires? Ties with Europe had strengthened the island and created trade, but it also had created the endless wars with France and the Netherlands. It had created a world in which the aristocrats of England had to deal with the revolutionaries of France and America. What could Copenhagen offer that London could not?

A smile crossed her face as she remembered their discussions. William seemed to be sure it was necessary, and so it was necessary. She was his partner in marriage and the labs, but money and business were solely his domain.

William joined them a moment later, escorting her best friend and honorary sister, Valeria on his arm. She let go and rushed over to Nora.

"You should have come aboard, Nora. It is extraordinary. I wanted to see the engines so your William bribed a fellow to show us around. They are remarkable, huge pistons and furnaces. They look like they were built for use by much larger beings than ourselves. Maybe the demons out of Milton's *Pandemonium*."

Nora smiled to herself, knowing what would come next. Valeria had memorised so much of what she had read word for word. Nora noted it as one of the differences between the two women. Nora always ensured she remembered the shortest, most succinct version of whatever she read. Valeria on the other hand seemed to attend to the exact detail of the words used.

Valeria was still going on about "Our purer essence" which had by that point been assumed to have evolved, allowing the demons to "overcome their noxious vapour, or inured not to feel."

As Valeria continued Nora hoped that this would be true for her too. That this absence of William would fade or she too would become "inured not to feel".

Valeria paused her recitation and looked Nora up and down.

"Do not look so sad, Nora," she said.

"Good Lord, Valeria," Nora replied. "How can I not with you reciting long passages from Milton and describing my husband's ship as a place of Hell."

"It is just a story; besides, they will only be gone a little while and I will be here to keep you company, and you will be here to keep me from fretting over Allen."

William stepped forward and placed a hand on Nora's stomach. She loved that, it calmed her. There was something about feeling his hand on the outside and his child's hand pressing up from inside her. It made her feel less like Nora the orphan, and more like Mrs Richmond, one part of three in the Richmond family.

The baby kicked a little, and Nora coughed on the smoke and the stink of the river and wondered if all this might in some way be poisoning her child.

In the labs at home William had been dissecting unborn animals that had developed wrong. Though she loved his scientific mind and knew he was doing valuable work, at the moment she hated this so much. She could picture the horror of a monkey foetus, four eyes closed against the horror of its own existence. The other two snake foetuses William had been dissecting that week had been perfectly formed, but the third and smallest had two heads.

Occasionally, Nora had nightmares about the baby inside her coming out with two heads, or coated in scales, or with a horrible tumour like the larger of the three snakes. These dreams were terrifying and would leave her feeling scared and angry about nothing in particular for days and days after they occurred.

William's new project had extended from the cataloguing of pre-natal mammals to a wider assessment of development in vertebrates. To help, she had spent more time than she cared to in the formaldehyde stinking animal lab, helping him carve up his baby monsters.

The baby kicked again, reassuring her with its strength of movement and vigorousness. It was healthy, she was just worried because she would be alone for some weeks. Everything would be fine. *Everything* would be fine.

"Everything will be fine," William said, leaning forward and kissing her gently on the lips.

She smiled, this time with conviction. The echo of his words and her thoughts gave the phrase a feeling of fateful significance for her, that reassured her nauseated gut that it must be a truth.

"Everything will all be okay," she agreed. "Just a matter of weeks and then you will be back."

Why do I still feel so unsure of your return? she wondered silently to herself.

She looked at Valeria who was talking in hushed tones with Allen. Their signs of affection were necessarily less obvious than Nora's own. Valeria was still a maid. The gold band on her own third finger told the world that her and William's romance was a love sanctioned by God and the law. Allen and Valeria had to make do with briefly held hands when out in public like this.

At least, that was how Valeria seemed to act. The truth was, neither Nora, Allen nor Valeria were all that sure of what polite society did. Every single thing they knew about "correct" behaviour and good manners had been taught to them by the odious Miss June. The orphanage owner's puritanism could never be questioned, but she might not have been the best authority in the world on the social mores of the upper-crust of the aristocracy.

A smile came to her face. William wouldn't mind, even though to him the manners of these people were like water to a fish. He'd lived in this world so long that he knew by instinct rather than book learning what fork to pick up for what course, and which was the correct form of address to use when conversing with a countess. And — of course

— how two young unmarried love birds should comport themselves under the watchful eye of Johnny Public. Despite all this William didn't care what people did only what they were and he saw that Nora, Valeria, and Allen were good at heart and she loved him for that as much as anything else.

Nora worried how hard this time would be on Valeria. Her relationship with Allen was intense, Nora could tell that, but it was also brittle. Their pasts were difficult. Allen's betrayal had been forgiven but not completely forgotten and both she and Valeria were aware of the stories of unattached men in foreign ports.

In fact, they had seen plenty of evidence of such from the carriage windows on the journey down to the *Catherine the Great*. Though they had politely ignored the huge population of prostitutes that stood on street corners and outside the kind of inn that would rent you an upstairs room for a half hour along with your pint of stout.

They had also seen sailors in a fist fight. The rougher elements of society were out in force, and in daylight too. Perhaps Valeria's worries about the judgement of society could have been reserved for a more refined crowd than the dock workers, sailors, and their prostitutes who were really all that remained on their quay now.

"I will miss you so much," William said pulling her mind back to the terrible present.

"I will miss you too, my love."

"I will have so much to tell you and I will write every day. I can't wait to describe the eclipse and the feeling of night's power over day."

Nora nodded and smiled to hide her sorrow. William was hoping to catch an eclipse as it passed over Denmark. Nora knew that in many ways this was the true reason why he was packing up and heading over there, instead of deputising someone and sending them instead. There were plenty of people at the Athenaeum Club and the Royal Society that could have dealt with this absurd trip. They knew his designs, understood them, and they could have conducted business on his behalf easily enough. But William would not pass up the opportunity to do some science in person, so she would wait at home and tend his experiments while he braved the open ocean.

He had told her how in many primitive societies an eclipse was a sign of bad things to come. He had laughed, but the fact had cut Nora to the quick and, she suspected, contributed to her general sense of non-specific dread.

It all added up to create Nora's feeling that something terrible was coming for them. That this trip might turn out badly.

Allen being with William gave her some relief. This was more his world than William's. He was capable, streetwise and able to look after himself... and William. Allen had shown considerable skill in the technical arts, helping William out with his experiments and tools. With William recently incorporating a company to manage his various patents and ventures, Allen had been raised up from employee to business partner. He even held shares in William's company.

Yes, Allen would keep William from wandering into danger or total ruination.

It did not help to tell herself these things though. Still the shadow of fate would not shift, as physical a presence for Nora as the shadow of the *Catherine the Great*.

Somewhere in the bowels of the ship they heard a rumble start up, the trickle of smoke from its twin stacks began to build into a thicker, blacker billow.

"We best be going," William said, pulling away from Nora.

As she looked up at his face his eyes lingered, not on her face, but on the swell of her pregnant belly.

"I will miss you," she said.

"I will miss you too, my love."

Valeria and Allen were saying similar goodbyes. The moment felt like it should have more import than these few words and then Allen and William were gone and walking up the plank as the engines within the machine built up a head of steam to power its huge wheel.

The men disappeared and Nora lingered for a while hoping to see the boat sail away, but Valeria grabbed her arm and pulled her away.

"I cannot bear to watch them go," Valeria said.

Nora could not say anything, the words she wanted to say stuck in her throat behind some trap door that seemed to have fallen across it.

It will be fine, she said to herself, but the voice within her had an echo that repeated its old mantra from the days after her wedding. *It cannot last.*

The midday gun fired and her heart hammered against her chest. *It cannot last, it cannot last.*

She did not turn when she heard the boat behind them let out a hoot and the grinding of the massive gears got underway. Steam was expanding, applying force to pistons, rods to turn it to rotation… she could picture clearly all the mechanics of the steam engine. She had seen endless diagrams in William's books. He often said that to understand a terrible thing robbed it of all power. To know the psychology of those who had witnessed ghosts was to destroy the haunting power of hauntings. To know that disease was not a random visitation from an angry pagan god, but a microbe that could be fought, washed away, or burned up was to rob the sickly of their horror.

But knowing all the parts of the engine behind her did nothing to dissipate the gut-wrenching fear as it pulled her beloved away from here and out into the cold, deep waters of the North Sea and the unknowable foreigners of the Scandinavian peninsula. She dreaded to think what manner of female seductress stalked the ports of Europe, what manner of violent men. So, she allowed herself to be pulled through the muck and brutishness of London's docks out onto the road where they hailed a cab to take them back to the house off Baker Street.

2

Stephen's usually stoic face was almost showing a smile on the ladies' return to the house. Valeria smiled to herself. Whenever Mr Richmond was away Stephen could attempt to bring the order he craved to the upstairs rooms. Those rooms which he — by agreement with Mr Richmond — entered only briefly and with eyes averted from the mess and grubbiness which Mr Richmond's work caused the labs to be in constantly.

He was already hung with dusting cloths like he was a clothesline. The butler/ come house steward/ come valet/ come housekeeper was in such a hurry to get back to his work that he dropped Valeria's bonnet twice and then a number of dust cloths each time he bent down to pick the bonnet up.

Valeria took her bonnet from him and hung it beneath the stairs herself, guiding Nora to the stairs and walking her up to her room. Nora had been almost completely silent on their walk home, where Valeria had been bursting to talk.

As the carriage had rattled over the cobbles, she had felt some pressure building within her. Like, she imagined, the way steam must build in the belly of a ship like the *Catherine Something*.

What was its name, she wondered? She had been so tied up in Allen, in writing every detail of his face into her memory, along with the texture of his hands when he held hers. All of it was documented as minutely as the lab notes she had seen Nora taking for Mr Richmond.

She could ask Nora. Nora would know about the workings of an engine like the *Catherine Whatsit*. Nora was a sponge for this stuff now, mopping up after her husband and filling up with knowledge, the way Valeria felt in the carriage.

It was a feeling that something needed to be said, some mark made of the occasion, or perhaps just some conversation struck up to fill the silence. No matter what Valeria had asked or declaimed, Nora had remained silent but a for a few short responses of the "Yes" and "No" variety.

Such distress in her friend and saviour was too much.

Stephen was busy, he would talk, but first Nora must be cared for.

Clearly, this had all been too much for the pregnant lass. She was absolutely glowing yesterday, today she looked half dead. Worried sick. Quite literally, she looked green about the gills as if they were on that *Catherine Something* on a rough sea.

Nora thanked Valeria sweetly for looking after her. For taking her up to her bed and helping with taking off her boots, coat, dress, and bonnet, and for getting her comfortably into bed. It was only after Nora had insisted that she was fine and would Valeria please and thank you go away, that Valeria headed to the labs and sought Stephen out.

Working in the labs was ideal for Valeria. Although, she did not understand the science that was being done around her. With Nora in bed and therefore in no shape to help her understand, she was still more than qualified to get stuck in with Stephen's tidying efforts.

For a moment she thought back over her life. Years of hard work cleaning, tidying, washing, cooking, and all manner of other menial tasks in the dreadful orphanage, had calloused her hands and knees and given her the instinct for domestic order. Then she had been so lucky to become the companion of Deloris Umbridge at her wonderful townhouse. How she missed the old woman who had once thought of her as a daughter.

A flash of anger pushed away her sadness. Though she had forgiven Allen for breaking into her home it still hurt. The rift he had caused between her and Deloris was heart-breaking and it had once more seen her on the streets. Only a chance encounter with Nora had saved her. Caught begging at the market by Nora she had been brought back here and reintroduced to Allen by her dear old friend. To find out that Nora was so happily married would have been enough but Nora offered her a home. Though she was told to behave as a guest she worked as hard as she could to earn her keep and she had never been happier.

Soon she had found out that Allen had robbed Delores's house to save her. Threats had been made and he had no choice. The two had grown close once more, only now Allen was gone. Off on this voyage and adventure and she missed him already. Putting in some work would help take her mind off the man with the jet-black hair and bright blue eyes that she knew she loved.

Luckily, Stephen was a meticulous taskmaster so Valeria was never without clear instructions, nor tasks to complete.

Together the two of them scrubbed their way through the chemical glassware, mucked out the biological cages, ordered the bookshelves, the chemical store, the formaldehyde jars full of strange specimens. They dusted the telescopes, mopped the floors and swept up the sawdust and metal filings around the bench Allen used to make replacement parts for various bits of equipment.

It was good to have a distraction, Valeria found. Without Allen there to pass the time she was lost.

When, about a week later the labs were done, she found herself at a loose end. *I wish that I had access to a proper library*, she thought.

There were plenty of books in the house, but they were full of the kind of technical jargon only William and Nora really understood, and were all on topics about which Valeria had no knowledge and little interest. She longed for something with a good debate in it: politics, art criticism, theories of history. The kind of books that Deloris had in huge quantities.

She shook her head, that was foolish thinking. You can't go back in time. *At least not if I remember my Augustine properly.* What was all that about cycles and arrows and...? If only she had a copy of *City of God* to consult. A sad smile crossed her face, there would have been one in Deloris' library.

With some irritation Valeria went to find Nora.

Nora had worried her after the boat left with William and Allen on it, but she seemed to calm herself after a few days. At first, she was quiet, pale, and would hardly eat a thing. Now she was more like herself and Valeria was so pleased. The thought of anything happening to her dear friend was more than she could bear.

After that, Valeria would sit with Nora and they would talk about nothing in particular. Nora would sew and knit. Usually, it was little clothes for the baby, but she had also knitted a blanket for Valeria and small tokens and gifts for those around her. Like tidying the labs, Valeria could see that sewing and knitting gave Nora something to do with her hands and her mind.

For Valeria it was fun to rediscover these feminine pastimes with Nora. Nora had been so long wrapped up in the work of Mr Richmond, and indeed her own modest researches which were often appended to her husband's. This was so they could be read at the Royal Society which did not let women into the building or to submit papers. Nor did the Royal Society have any intention of changing this anytime soon.

With Nora out of the labs to avoid exposing the baby to any of the dangerous chemicals, animal diseases, or heavy instruments Nora had been on a largely self-imposed hiatus from anything even smelling of natural philosophy.

To keep her mind sharp, she spoke with Valeria about the softer subjects, art, politics, history, which Valeria felt were more her speed thanks to Miss Umbridge's crash courses and reading lists.

On the day the knock came to their door, however, they were both involved in the most frivolous of reminiscences.

"I wonder," Nora said, "what is happening back at the orphanage."

Valeria's smiled faded from her lips and her stomach felt cold, tight, like she had swallowed something foul tasting. "I do not know," she offered. "But I fear Miss June was never on a path to redemption. I cannot imagine her becoming less herself. Less awful and cruel."

"I have hope," Nora said.

"You always do."

A look of sadness flashed across Nora's face,

catching Valeria's attention. There was a pause before Nora opened her mouth and said, hesitantly, "I wish that were true. Do you not remember what it is to have no hope?"

"Remember? Of course, I lived in the same squalid orphanage as you, Nora. I remember waking up and knowing I would never be adopted. That I would never leave that place except to go somewhere worse — the workhouse, or the grave."

"I do not think that is true." Nora had such a strange expression on her face when she said this that Valeria held back the angry response that seemed to press against her lips.

"I do not mean that you did not suffer, or suffered less than me. I just... it is so hard to put these things into words. There should be a scientific description of feelings, something precise and measurable, a language I can use to explain, without sounding so rude to you."

"Nora, I know you do not mean to upset me. We have time this afternoon, why not try to create that language. The beginnings of that science."

Nora laughed. "I suppose what I mean is that there is a feeling so much darker than sadness, so much worse than the day to day hopelessness. I know that I believed every day in that orphanage was hopeless until I really, truly had lost all hope. Do you see what I mean? If there is no hope, there is no more reason to keep living. Except perhaps for fear of death."

Valeria understood now and her heart reached out to Nora, but she did not know what to say.

Suicide! she thought, was Nora talking about suicide? It was a mortal sin. Neither the Pope's church, nor the Queen's would bury a suicide on sacred ground. The Catholics believed such people went to hell. It was one of the only truly irredeemable sins. Once committed your time was done, there was no opportunity for repentance.

When had her friend felt like this? She wanted to ask. But something held her back, some fear she could not quite name, but she believed it must be a Christian fear.

"It was after I first worked here," Nora said, answering the question that Valeria had left unasked. "Miss June believed Mr Richmond had seduced me—"

"Had he... not?"

"Not in the way Miss June believed. Not carnally."

"Go on."

"Miss June took me back to the orphanage and

all of a sudden I lost all my hope. All of it. She punished me, more cruelly than I had seen her punish any girl before. I was colder, more bruised, more alone than before, and worse still... I had seen what kind of life I might have. I had known kindness. Working in a house like this alongside Stephen, and in the presence of William, I had been shown the promised land. Not just from a mountain top like Moses but up close. I had drunk from the rivers of milk and honey and now I was back in the desert. And it was worse than when I left it. I planned to kill myself, Valeria. That is what it is to be without hope."

Valeria took her hand and they sat in silence for a while, then, like the sun coming out from behind a cloud, the room cheered up. It was as if both of them had realised at the same moment that all that was behind them. That some modicum of hope would always remain, because they had come through all they had come through and were still here, still happy. With men they loved in their lives, and a warm house to live in, and a beautiful future laid out ahead of them.

They began to talk lightly again, telling jokes and stories, remembering only the good moments and imagining moments even better than those.

Valeria was laughing at one of Nora's stories when the knock came.

The visitor had completely ignored the doorbell, either out of ignorance or carelessness, and the knock was timid enough that Stephen, still elbow deep in a sink full of scientific glassware upstairs, had no hope of hearing it.

Valeria got up and went to see who it was, leaving Nora sat in the shafts of morning sunlight from the window through which Allen had come back into their life.

She was a little surprised to realise that this was a task she had not done since she had walked out of Miss Umbridge's home all those months ago. It gave her a pang of guilt, thinking of the old woman bedridden and living in the house she had presided over for so long, with no more power of presiding.

She wondered how awful Thomas Wright might have made the place in her absence. She remembered his transformation from the everyman lawyer to the condescending and hard head of a household so much wealthier than he could ever hope to be, no matter how well the lawyering trade treated him.

She was still thinking of this when she opened the door and came face to face with Delores's cook, Cookie. She was speechless for a moment.

"Good afternoon, Miss Collins. Mr Wright has sent me round to fetch you. He has a matter of great importance to speak with you about."

Valeria's voice came back to her putting her into a state of shock. "My goodness, Cookie. But how on earth did you — did that man find me?"

"Might I tell you on the way, Miss. The master said it was a most urgent matter."

Valeria's heart sank. She knew immediately what it was. Had known it the second she saw Cookie.

"I will get my bonnet and cape," she said.

3

Stepping into Miss Umbridge's house had the same creepy significance on Valeria's nerves as entering an empty church. It was so familiar as to feel like home, which for several years it had been, and yet all the emotional associations were wrong. It made the place feel like a ghost house, taking on some alluring form but failing to convey the soul of the thing.

Cookie shut the door behind them and Valeria expected the heavy thump to lift dust off this uninhabited place, but of course it did not. It was not uninhabited. Just because she had abandoned it, did not make it an abandoned house.

She stood in the hall with Cookie a little while, trying to reacclimatise, waiting for the feeling of

THE MAID'S BLESSING

being caught off guard, surrounded by an unseen but ever-present danger.

She had known, the moment she opened the door of Nora's house and saw Cook standing there on the stoop. She had known it so surely; she could have delivered the news herself.

Instead she had curtseyed out of habit and asked Cookie why she was there.

The answer was as she expected, that she had known — Miss Umbridge was dead.

What other disaster could have caused that house to come hurtling back into her orbit, like one of the recurring comets Mr Richmond was forever trying to catch sight of through the London smog?

She did not invite Cookie in, did not ask for details, did not even tell Nora she was going. She simply took her bonnet and cloak down from the pegs on which they hung beneath the stairs and followed Cookie out into the street.

And here she was back under Miss Umbridge's roof. This was a house of death, the body had gone but Miss Umbridge remained in possession. The will had been read but no paperwork had been drawn up yet, no deeds transferred or money doled out. Mr Wright would not allow it until he had held a number of meetings, and Valeria was to be the first of them.

All Cookie had said was that Mr Wright wanted to see her and that it was part of his duties as executor. Cookie had seemed older. There was grey in her hair now and she seemed thinner. The account she gave of the house was of a death by a thousand tiny cuts. Mr Wright had taken an iron hold, and punished the staff liberally since Valeria had left. She had stung his sense of manhood when she rejected his marriage proposal.

"He is in the library, Miss Collins," Cookie said.

Valeria withdrew a little, the strange formality of "Miss Collins" after years of being "Valeria", or "Miss", or "You" made her uneasy and added to the feeling that this was a dream where nothing familiar could be entirely trusted. Nodding, she made her way down the main hallway and through to the library. There was a shiny new handle on the door, one with a keyhole where before there had been none. She turned the handle and the mechanism gave out a small squeak of well-oiled metal, but beyond that, was completely silent.

She shivered again and pushed her way in past the door.

The library was almost entirely as she remembered it. The huge walls of books. The only thing she noted was that the gap-toothed shelves were now seamless, every book in the house had been returned to its proper place. The piles in her old room, in Miss Umbridge's, in the drawing rooms and on small side tables throughout the house had all been placed back on the shelves in their rightful place.

Where Miss Umbridge's old desk had stood — the desk that Allen had broken into in order to rob Miss Umbridge and appease the now gaoled Taylor — there was now a much larger desk. It had been brought downstairs from the main office and piled high with log books, pocketbooks, notebooks, ledgers, and loose papers of every kind and colour. It gave the room the appearance of a cathedral in a sect devoted to the written word.

Behind this alter, like a priest of letters, sat Mr Wright. He did not look up right away but continued with his entry in the open ledger in front of him. In the past Valeria would have waited through this silence, experienced this silence as the assertion of power it was meant to be.

But she was not here as a cowed servant and a young girl. She was a free woman, a guest in this house who could and would leave when she cared to, and had nothing to fear from this petty dictator.

She turned and walked into the library rounding a shelf stack and entering the reading nook where a second fireplace sat, unlit. She browsed the shelves looking for the volume of Decline and Fall of the Roman Empire that she had read before she left. The one describing the court of Attila the Hun during his rise to becoming a sacker of Augustus' marble city. She found it and taking a seat beside the fireplace, began to read. It took a few minutes before she heard Mr Wright slam his blotter down on the paper and rise to come and find her. He rounded the corner and Valeria could see from the corner of her eye that he was struggling to hide his irritation at having lost this opening salvo in whatever negotiating was to be done.

He seemed to gain his composure and, in an attempt to salvage the upper hand, bowed to her, and said in a cheerful voice, as if no bad blood had ever passed between them, "Miss Collins, thank you for waiting for me."

Valeria continued to read until the end of the page then closed the book.

"No, my dear Mr Wright, thank you for waiting for me. I have so missed having access to a library with the breadth of Miss Umbridge's. Please take a seat."

Seeing no way to ignore this request without being impolite, Mr Wright obeyed, sitting opposite her and eyeing her up with a quizzical expression on his face.

I too must seem oddly familiar, yet different, Valeria thought to herself.

"You may well have reason to rejoice then. This library is part of why you are here. I have asked you here because—"

"I imagine this has to do with Miss Umbridge's estate," Valeria cut him off. She wondered what the remark about the library meant, perhaps she had been given some of the books, or else access to the library in Miss Umbridge's will? She wanted him to go on, but was determined not to let him lead the conversation. "I am more concerned about the woman than her belongings, Mr Wright. When did she pass?"

She was careful in her tone not to overstep, but could tell he was rankled by the change in the power dynamic. So long as she was not outright rude to him, however, there was nothing he could do to her anymore.

"She passed on Friday. Was buried yesterday. No, the day before, Sunday. She was very sick at the time and her passing was as peaceful as we all hoped.

She was not showing any sign of improvement from her apoplexy."

Suddenly, it hit her. Until then she had been hiding behind the idea that there was never any hope for Deloris, that all this was inevitable. Now she remembered that Deloris was not all gone before the end. That she could have returned, could have spoken to the woman who saved her from Miss June. The one who had educated her, shown her possibilities beyond the limits of her birth, her wealth, and her gender.

"I am very sorry to hear all this. Our friendship was under a lot of strain before I left this house," Valeria said. "But she was a kind woman, and I loved her very dearly."

"It transpires that she loved you too. Despite, as you say, the strain of your relationship."

She noted that he could not bring himself to describe her as a friend of the old woman, and so she diverted him once more from his purpose. Frustrating him gave her a brief moment of spiteful satisfaction, of which she was not proud.

"Tell me, Mr Wright. How did you know where to send your cook to find me?"

At this he perked up and a wide smile crossed his lips.

Damn it, Valeria thought. *This is a victory for him, rooting me out of my hiding place.*

"Mrs Richmond and I rely on the same butcher to supply our kitchens. It is, I understand, quite a distance for both our households, but there really is no better a supplier of beef in the city. One of the maids recognised you with your new charitable patroness and when word got back to me, I had her follow you. I felt it was useful information to have, and now that Miss Umbridge has passed and I am to execute her last will and testament, I am proven right."

"I take it then that I am included in her wishes."

"Very much so. With the exception of a number of charitable donations, gifts to all her staff and their families, and the settling of several of her estates on those distant relatives she anticipated would most annoy her close relatives, the largest portion of her estate, this house and its contents included have been passed on to me."

"I still do not see what this has to do with me, Mr Wright. I would appreciate you coming to the point."

"Well, Miss Collins — Valeria, the relevance is this: well over half the value of the portion allotted to me is to be held in trust by the bank until such time as I am married—"

"This again, was I unclear the first time? Have you forgotten how you behaved after I gave you my answer? You put me out on to the streets to beg my way to the poorhouse. Is there no other scullery maid for you to try and work your mastery over?"

"To take your questions in the reverse order in which they were levelled at me, I have no interest in any other scullery maid. I am, and have been for the longest time, in love with you. I have never regretted anything more than what happened. It was... in a fit of rage brought on by painful disappointment, that I cast you out of my life."

"I am so sorry to have caused you such sorrow," Valeria snapped.

"You appear to have found yourself a comfortable situation, I never doubted your ability to look after yourself."

"Then what incentive can you offer me to make me let you look after me? Marriage for my gender is little more than servant-ship without pay or hope of escape. And I am not in need of a new employer."

"If pay is all you are worried about, then you have your answer to your first question — I can offer you vast wealth. Marry me and you are mistress of this house. The additional money will keep you and everyone you love comfortable for the rest of their lives. But I hope I can offer more as a husband than the size of my estates."

"What might that be? Your cruelty? I have been ruled over by the cruel before and have no wish to spend any more time in the grip of those too weak to protect those they have power over. And you are too weak to protect your wards from even your own small villainy."

She managed to say all this in the even and polite tone that they had been conducting the whole conversation in.

He opened his mouth to speak. "Without your hand in marriage, I cannot access my full inheritance. Without my hand, you cannot access any of yours at all. Miss Umbridge saw me as a fine match for you. This is a dying woman's last wish."

"I see you have learned from last time that anger achieves nothing. This grovelling and bargaining are perhaps even less attractive. I am in love with another man. A man I would never have seen again, and probably have hated all my life if you had not driven me out of this house and into his arms, Mr Wright. Now that Miss Umbridge is dead and you have informed me of my part in her will, I believe there is no reason for us to ever speak a single word to one another again."

Mr Wright looked utterly crestfallen. She could see him formulating his arguments as if he were in court. Running each one by a mental jury and trying to find one that might persuade them. Valeria stood up and left him there still thinking about the problem. He knew as surely as she did that there was no reasoning with her.

He was done.

It was with a sense of closure that she shut the library door behind her. The lock that used to make such a loud bang now slid shut and held the door closed without a sound, closing off the past, she hoped, for good.

4

Allen eyed the clouds with growing anxiety. The air had that electric feel that builds before a storm. The wind was picking up that instant and cold, and the clouds confirmed it all. They covered the sky in a blanket of grey that darkened to a near pitch black out at the horizon. The blackness was intermittently broken up by flashes of lightning deep within the clouds.

He held the railing tighter than he needed to. The boat was handling the chop well, but he knew it would take one rough squall from the wrong angle and the steady roll could come to a crashing halt. The sails were being hauled down behind him, leaving the mast bare and putting all the strain on the huge paddle and the steam engine that drove it.

It would be slow going, but they would lose much less ground than they might tacking back and forth into the wind. Below him, over the railings he could see the strange patterns of foam that violent winds left on the surface of the water and could taste the tang of salt sea spray on his tongue.

He did not want to say anything to William, who appeared wholly unperturbed by the weather, but he was terrified. The sea was a horror he was ill-equipped to deal with. He had been raised in a city where there was no skyline to speak of. When he looked up from one of London's streets, he was hemmed in by the multi-story terraces put up to house factory workers by the thousands. That thin strip of sky overhead was his horizon. To see far meant a mile or so of broken scenery across the hills on the edge of town or down one of the longer straits of the river. Out here he could see the dome of the sky right down to where it met the sea. The horizon was unbroken and flat. He was a speck in a whole cosmos of unknowable fury. And now, he felt, this angry god of distance was coming to wreak an impersonal punishment on him and the crew of the huge ship they were on.

Mr Richmond, on the other hand, was unworried by the vastness of the world. His was a childhood of rolling fields and seaside holidays. Besides, to him there was no mystery in the power of the storm. It was a function, so he had told Allen, of the laws of thermodynamics as codified in the last century by some of the greatest minds since Newton.

The warm water, evaporating into the sky carries with it all the energy of the sun... or was it the energy of the earth, geo-something heat? Either way, that heat then fuelled the wind by a process of — what was the word? Convection, conduction...?

He found that William's explanations comforted him only so long as they stayed in his head. He had understood it all as William spoke, but like a dream, the moment the explanation was done it began to fade from his mind.

It was the words that made it hard. So many new words, alien to his tongue. Words that had travelled; they came from Greece and ancient Rome. From the maps he had seen he understood these were even further than Copenhagen which had seemed like another planet to him. The people there a whole other species; tall, blonde, elf-like. They made him feel even more common than his new circle in London.

It would be good to get back, he thought. Good to get home and see all the familiar sights, smell the familiar smells... perhaps not the Thames, which would be especially foul-smelling at this time of year.

But to see Valeria again, that would be lovely, he could picture her smile, the way she would look at him when he arrived. He loved that. The way she made him feel seen.

The rumble of thunder reached the boat, and he shivered. It would be with them in an hour or so. The thunder was persistent. It would be the sort that rattled windows.

Electricity, he thought. Something like that. William had explained that too. Electricity and lightning, and somehow it made the light and sound.

He would ask when he got back to their cabin. William had barely left there since they had settled in a few days ago. He had been hit by a bout of seasickness almost immediately on leaving the port.

Closing the door behind him had made him feel better, so he had turned the heavy handle to bolt it shut. Inside the boat, if it were not for the rolling motion, he could be walking the corridors of a London hotel, having come in through the window. Some instinct in him left over from his childhood had him looking about for signs of hotel staff who might throw him out.

If it really were like that, he thought, *I would be*

looking to rob people like me. To slip into rooms like mine, to pilfer from the bags of people like me, those who could afford to live in rooms paid for by the night.

He was one of those people now. Or at the very least, the employee of one of those people. What a stark difference it was from being under the thumb of someone like Taylor. Or working for himself, scurrying up and down the streets in hopes of lifting enough to eat, to live.

He took the stairs down a level, and caught sight of a flash of lightning through a porthole.

One... two— the crash of thunder came almost immediately on two.

So, about two miles to go, he thought. That was close. The boat could do ten or twelve knots. Say ten for ease. That meant ten or twenty minutes before the storm was right overhead. It would start raining soon.

The lightning and the memories of the streets of London reminded him of a play Mr Richmond had taken Nora, Valeria and himself to. There had been a king and a madman and a line had stuck in Allen's head the way the scientific words of William simply would not. The king had said to the beggar:

"Is man no more than this? Consider well. You owe the worm no silk, the beast no hide, the sheep no wool, the cat no perfume. Here's three sophisticated people, but you art the thing itself. Unaccommodated man is no more than such a poor, bare, forked animal as you."

He had not understood everything, though Valeria had told him the story beforehand, but he had understood that moment, had felt the meaning of those words, "unaccommodated man, a poor, bare, forked animal." He understood because those words described what he had been. Someone with nothing to his name, no home to speak of, and no wool, silk, or perfume. And now here he was, position reversed, one of the sophisticated people like the king. With home and love and work.

There were nights on the street when he would have been happy to die, to move on to whatever came next because it could have been no worse than living in the filth and the muck, and waiting for men like Taylor to decide if his fate was food or starvation.

In the cabin William was lying on his bunk reading from the book Valeria had given him. A beautiful, illustrated copy of a book by an American author. When he came in, William smiled and started reading aloud.

"Why did the old Persians hold the seas holy? Why did the Greeks give it a separate deity, and own brother of Jove? Surely all this is not without meaning, and still deeper the meaning of that story of Narcissus, who because he could not grasp the tormenting, mild image he saw in the fountain, plunged into it and was drowned. But that same image, we ourselves see in all rivers and oceans. It is the image of the ungraspable phantom of life; and this is the key to it all." He propped himself up and looked at Allen. "Good stuff, eh?"

Allen did not like the word "drowned", it spoke a little too directly to his worries, but he smiled as best he could and said, "Aye, Mr Richmond. 'Good stuff' indeed."

William fell back on the bed. "Truth be told, Allen, I am sick as a dog, I have been since we left port."

Allen did his best to sound surprised. "You hide it well, Sir."

"What I would not give for Nora being here to run her fingers through my hair and to calm my brow."

Allen had not considered this particular act of intimacy and imagined Valeria with those delicate fingers ploughing parallel furrows in his hair. That did seem like it would be nice. But his feelings were not of comfort as he imagined this, but of fear.

Once he had been an unaccommodated man. Now, he had something to lose, and as they barrelled on towards the storm, he was terrified of death because Valeria would not be there on the other side if he were to, like Narcissus, plunge into the mirror of the fountain and drown.

5

The dock records showed that the *Catherine the Great* ran back and forth from London to Oslo twice while William Richmond and Allen were in Denmark.

The ship went north to Oslo first then doubled back via first, Copenhagen then Haarlem just outside Amsterdam, then onwards to Antwerp, Calais, and London. Then back to Oslo by the same route. It was on the *Catherine the Great*'s third trip, with William and Allen both aboard that it completely vanished on its leg between the Kingdom of Denmark and the Kingdom of the Netherlands.

The agent for the owner of the *Catherine the Great* in Haarlem, allowed the usual three days for delays then wired Antwerp and Copenhagen for any news. The boat had left on time from Copenhagen and had not shown up in Antwerp. So, it had not bypassed Haarlem.

The agent, who was a man paid to worry about things on behalf of others, took another day interviewing captains who had come in along the same shipping lane, then he interviewed those coming in on more or less direct lanes in case the ship got off course. No sign could be found, though they did report unseasonably bad weather in the Kattegat — the straits between Sweden and Denmark.

So, with his suspicions more or less confirmed, the agent contacted the harbourmaster in Haarlem.

The harbourmaster in Haarlem wired his counterpart on the London docks, where the paperwork on the *Catherine the Great* said it was registered.

The harbourmaster in London then contacted Lloyd's of London, who underwrote the insurance on the *Catherine the Great*. Lloyd's conducted their own checks taking up another day and a half telegraphing back and forth.

A busy trading lane like the North Sea was a hard place for a ship to vanish into, so the investigators at Lloyd's soon concluded that the ship was sunk or else stolen. If it were afloat, it would have been spotted. It took another few days to fill in the forms, negotiate a settlement with the owner and arrange payment.

With the insurance company having confirmed the owner's fears, the passenger manifest was dug up and telegrams sent to the addresses of all who left addresses notifying the passenger's families of their loved one's disappearances. This was conducted by the owner after the ship had been missing for two full weeks.

※

Valeria heard the bell pull clunk as someone pulled it at the door, and deep within the servant's quarters there came the tinkling of the bell. She was sat in the drawing room pulling needle and thread through a complex cross-stitch pattern, beside her was the copy of Gibbon's *Rise and*

Fall, which she had walked out of Miss Umbridge's house with.

After the shock of seeing Cookie and hearing the news of Miss Umbridge's death on the doorstep, she had avoided answering the door again. She feared — with what she recognised as the foolishness of the superstitious — that somehow bad news would arrive every time she went to the door.

So, she waited, listening to the pad of one of the maid's shoes in the hall, the unlocking of the door and a boy's voice saying, "Telegram for Mrs Richmond."

A moment later the maid came in. She curtseyed. "Sorry to bother you, Miss. I thought Mrs Richmond might be in here. There's a telegram for her."

Nora was upstairs, resting up. She would spend a couple of hours sleeping in the afternoons since William had left. In the two weeks since he was due back those naps had got longer and longer. She was going to bed earlier too, and waking up later. It was as if she were trying to shut out the world through unconsciousness. It made Valeria nervous and she spent much of the time reading up on prenatal health.

There was an appalling lack of it in the medical texts on William's shelves. It seemed that midwives were not as well published as most medical men, and they were all men.

"Give the telegram to me," Valeria said. "She's asleep at the moment, I'll take it up to her in a minute."

Valeria laid aside her cross-stitch and tucked the telegram into the book. She could not help but see the passage on the page *"The vicissitudes of fortune, which spares neither man nor the proudest of his works, buries empires and cities in a common grave."* Something about it reminded her of another quote from later in the book.

"His reign is marked by the rare advantage of furnishing very few materials for history; which is, indeed, little more than the register of the crimes, follies, and misfortunes of mankind."

Something about the echo of the word "fortune" — with its dual meanings of fate and wealth — troubled her.

Then she felt foolish. Here she was, looking for meaning in snatches of an old writer like those Orientals in a book she had read who left their every decision up to a book that was to be consulted by tossing a series of small flattened wooden rods. They claimed to read the future in whichever hexagram from the book that the rods indicated.

This is more of that superstitious thinking, she thought.

Then she put the book down and continued her cross-stitch until the clock chimed four o'clock and it was time to wake Nora from her peaceful slumbers.

Just then the door opened and Nora entered, wearing a dressing gown and her hair in disarray, the vast planet of her stomach jutting out ahead of her like the statues of fertility goddesses dug up in ancient German graves. She looked frightened, cradling her stomach protectively.

"My God, Nora," Valeria cried. "Whatever's the matter?"

"Oh, Valeria. I had the most awful dream."

The uneasiness took a hold of Valeria's stomach again and she glanced nervously at the book in which the unread telegram lay.

"Oh, Nora. I am sorry, but it is all over now. You're awake and you're safe. Sit down and tell me everything. I'll get Stephen to bring in some tea." She took another look at Nora's state of undress and corrected herself. "I'll get one of the girls to bring in some tea."

Once tea had been arranged and a girl despatched to the kitchen to set about the boiling and the brewing, Valeria returned and kneeled beside her friend's chair. Holding her hand, she asked, "What was it you dreamed?"

She was not sure she wanted to know; in fact, she knew that whatever it was Nora said, she was likely to read something into it as if Nora's sleep-addled thoughts were God's own gospel truth.

"I do not remember," Nora said. "But it was terrifying. I think it was to do with Baby."

She touched her stomach again, carefully but thoroughly, as if scientifically testing the reality of her pregnancy.

Valeria chuckled and touched Nora's stomach too. The bump was warm and she could feel the movement of both bodies beneath the one skin.

"Baby's still here. Oh," she said remembering the telegram. "There was a telegram for you. Would you like me to read it to you? It might be from William."

Nora sat up a little, and smiled. "What are those two up to?" She said it as if she suspected that they were simply out late to dinner. And certainly, they may have extended their stay in Copenhagen. William had said if things went a particular way, he might have to stay on to hash out the contracts. But he had yet to send a letter and he was two weeks overdue.

Valeria got up and grabbed the telegram, tearing it open. The handwritten note was written in the clear block capitals that all telegram office workers were trained to deliver with remarkable uniformity.

She paused and read it silently.

TO MRS RICHMOND FROM C P SHIPPING BEGIN MESSAGE REGRET TO INFORM YOU THAT CATHERINE THE GREAT IS SUNK STOP MR RICHMOND ABOARD WITH SERVANT STOP BOTH PARTIES LOST AT SEA STOP OUR DEEPEST CONDOLENCES STOP PLEASE CONTACT LLOYDS OF LDN RE COMPENSATION STOP END MESSAGE.

Her blood ran cold. She could hear her heart beating in her ears and felt horribly close to fainting. Her hands were numb, her head spun.

This could not be true.

Both parties lost at sea, she thought. What horrible wording. Perhaps it was another servant, Allen might have stayed behind. She slumped back into her chair and reread the telegram again. She looked at Nora who had gone white as a sheet.

"What's wrong, Valeria? What is it? Is it from William?"

Valeria looked up and tried to formulate the words to describe the end of the world. They had both lost the dearest thing to them. Without William's protection they would be fair game for his extended family who loathed Nora for being a commoner, and still more for having a baby that mixed their bloodline with the gutter.

They had lost their loves and stood to be plunged back into the cesspit they had risen out of. They had both been so close to dying a pauper's death, alone in the cold, miserable world of the workhouse. Now that fate seemed to be very much back in their cards.

Even as the pragmatic parts of her mind traced over the future implications the rest of her mind could not stop imagining Allen in his bunk, being flung sideways as the waves capsized the boat.

Nora looked like she was drowning, too. She could see it was bad news, though even in that certainty she could not know how bad. So long as Valeria remained silent there was hope for Nora.

How could she tell Nora of this loss? She could hardly believe it herself. Every fibre of her being wanted this to be a lie, or a joke, or better yet a dream from which she could shortly awake. Then she could go and find the real Nora, hold her, gain some sort of comfort from her.

But there was no value in delaying. This was no dream, no way to wake up, and Nora had to know. Nora, whose face showed so much fear already.

"It's from the ship owners," she said eventually, hearing her voice cracking around each word. Tears hovered, ready to fall and blur up her vision. "William and Allen's boat, Nora. It sank. They were on board.

Valeria sat silently as she watched Nora's face show every sign of running through the same set of thoughts that had struck her own like a tidal wave. The disbelief at first, then the realisation that disbelief made no sense at all. That this could only be the truth, because no one would bother to tell so hurtful and destructive a lie.

Valeria could see Nora's face going pale, whiter and whiter, till she looked dead, a walking corpse, with the child still sending up a heartbeat from inside her.

Eventually Nora was able to make a noise, a barely whispered imprecation. "Oh, God."

Then she slumped sideways to the floor and Valeria dropped from her chair to try and catch her. She caught Nora's shoulder's before she could hit the floor but there was a sickening crack as Nora's head struck the corner of the side table on which Valeria's copy of Gibbon was perched.

For a moment Valeria feared the worst then Nora's eyes opened and she touched her head gently, looking about, confusion written on her face. She had only been out for a few seconds at most, but she looked as if, like Rip Van Winkle, she had slept for years. Her eyes were starting out of her head and her hand, when it reached for Valeria's, seemed to be grasping and weak.

"Come on, Nora," Valeria said as she lifted the pregnant woman into a chair.

"He's gone?" Nora asked. Then again with the full horror of the situation dawning on her. "He is gone."

"Yes." That was all Valeria could think to say. The naked, unadorned truth. "They both are."

Nora began to cry. It was as if a dam had broken, from the silence of shock to this, terrifying, elemental wailing. She did not sob, she screamed. Tears poured down her face and her hands began to pull at her hair and the front of her nightdress. It was terrifying to behold. In all her years of oppression and loss, Valeria had never seen anything quite like it. Her own grief seemed to fade away in the presence of this break-down. Valeria thought for a moment that Nora might reach out and strike or choke or gouge Valeria's face, then it seemed as though that terrifying capacity for violence might be turned inwards in some self-destructive act.

Nora's eyes rolled back into her head and she screamed up at the sky in pain.

Valeria, in a daze, stood up and looked around. In the last minute or so since Nora had begun to scream Stephen had come in.

There was a small cut on Nora's forehead where she had hit her head as she fell and Valeria could see a stain on Nora's dress where the cut had dripped. But as she looked at it, she realised it was too much blood.

"Oh, God. Nora. You're hurt. Where are you bleeding from?"

She leaned in to look closer and realised when she put her hand on the cushion of the chair there was blood where Nora sat. She looked at the red mark on her hand and turned to Stephen.

"Stephen," she said. "We need a doctor. Now."

"What is it?" Stephen asked. "What on earth is going on?"

"The baby, Stephen. There is something wrong with the baby. We need a doctor now."

6

While Stephen ran for the doctor, Valeria and the maids carefully lifted Nora to her feet. Her legs shook when she took her own weight, but with Valeria's support and the assistance of various household staff they were able to get her upstairs to the spare bedroom where they put layers of fresh linen and Valeria heated some water to wash her friend. The bleeding had stopped as suddenly as it started, but Nora remained pale and sweating.

As she watched the water beginning to steam, all Valeria could think of was the face of Miss Umbridge in the moments before her stroke, that same paleness, the febrile confusion and sweat. She remembered the weeks after the stroke, Miss

Umbridge's lack of responsiveness. Her difficulty speaking, or even swallowing.

It was too horrible, it could not happen to Nora.

But what if it did? a voice inside her said. *What if it does? Or what if she dies?*

She could not lose Nora too. It was too much. Allen gone down on the *Catherine the Great* and Nora going on the same day. She too felt the loss of William, the kind benefactor of herself and Allen. The man who had saved them all when so many others had passed up the chance over and over again, or else had chosen to stamp them down further.

She soaked the towel watching the way the ripples in the basin spread from the submerged cloth and rebounded from the side. That was what it was like. This storm destroys a boat and like ripples in a basin the effects rush out from there. The boat destroys two men. The loss of those men kills Nora, kills her child, makes Stephen unemployed, Valeria homeless, and then... who else?

There was no one else.

Without Nora she was all alone now.

Well then, she thought, pushing aside the fear of loss, the hollow pain in her stomach where Allen's death had ripped her in two. Well then, Nora must live.

THE MAID'S BLESSING

It distracted her, this new task. She did not know what to do to make it happen, but right now there was the simple task of hot towels. She would clean her friend up, keep her awake and soothe her until the doctor arrived. Then she would work out the next step.

One step at a time. That was how to do it. Not to get too far ahead of oneself. Just keep ploughing on, till your furrow is done, and when you reach the end you worry about turning the plough, working out where to go next.

The towels were almost scalding, but the pain was distracting too and she rushed back to Nora's bedside and sent the maids for drinking water, brandy. In the darkened room with the curtains pulled, she used the towels to wipe her friend's brow. Clean the blood from Nora's legs and groin. Then tucked her in, pulling up a chair so that she could hold Nora's hand.

Valeria tried to remember a story to tell Nora, but they were all too sad. She could only think of Ovid with his endless stories of loss and transformation, or of kings deposed like Richard II, lovers betrayed like Troilus and Cresseyde, or of murderers like the Spanish Tragedy. There seemed no story in all the books she'd read that did not seem too raw or relevant to soothe.

So, she began to sing, the first hymn that came to her mind.

"Amazing grace, how sweet the sound, that saved the wretch like me."

The first few notes, faltered, caught in her throat. But by the time she reached the phrase "I once was lost, but now am found," she had hit her stride. The concentration required to control her breath, to keep the time and melody of the piece, allowed her to drift from her own worries to the eternal ones of the song. Nora's hand was warm in hers, the thready beat of her heart seemed stronger as Valeria sang, though she knew the act was as much, if not more, for her own peace of mind than Nora's.

When she reached the final words of the song — "When we've been there ten thousand years, bright shining as the sun, we've no less days to sing God's praise than when we first begun." She felt exhausted, drained, but dare not stop. That thread of superstitious people told her now that her voice was keeping Nora going, the only way to keep her alive until the doctor came was to keep singing.

She began anew with a different hymn. "On Jordan's stormy banks I stand..."

Why are there so many hymns to reassure the singer of the comfort found in death? Valeria wondered as she reached the line about the "healthful shore".

It felt like hours passed with her barely pausing for breath.

"And did those feet in ancient times, walk upon England's pasture's green... When I survey the wondrous cross, on which the prince of glory died... Rock of ages, cleft for me... Love divine, all loves excelling..."

She did not even notice Stephen had returned until he touched her shoulder.

The look of pity and concern that replaced the usual look of abject fury on Stephen's face, told her everything she needed to know about her own appearance. She must look as frightful as Nora.

"Go have a lie-down, Miss Collins," he said. "When we have seen to Mrs Richmond, I will have the doctor come and check in on you."

"No," she began to say. "I have to stay with her, to look after her..."

But Stephen's insistent hands pulled her to her feet and pushed her towards the door where one of Nora's maids took her by the arm and frog-marched her to bed.

It was then, in the quiet of her own room, with Nora being looked after and nothing left to distract her that she allowed herself to fully consider the scale of her sorrow. To probe that hole left by Allen's destruction. The pain welled up within her and she was consumed, sinking down into it to the sound of her own sobbing. It sounded very far away; the way sounds above the surface sound when she sank below the surface of the water in her bath.

How would she survive such pain, how would she go on?

7

"Miss Collins," said the lawyer to Valeria. "I need you to calm Mrs Richmond, please. It is important that we address the full scope of Mr Richmond's will, and we cannot proceed if she continually causes this sort of disruption."

Nora was sobbing, deep hiccupping sobs which racked her whole body. She had barely been able to speak without breaking down into tears in the days since the telegram had arrived when she had collapsed completely.

Valeria had done all she could for her. The worry about the baby and about her friend's health was all that kept her going through her own grief and worry for the future. Even so, it had taken nearly a week just to get Nora well enough to leave her bed and come down to the drawing room. In that room, William's lawyer read the will and began the process of transferring the estate from William to his heirs. This final process brought everything back. Making things official legally just proved that the men were gone and there was no hope. Without a body to bury both of them had bounced from gut-wrenching grief to hope. A slim belief that this was all a mistake. Only now even that was taken from them and Valeria felt as if her stomach had dropped out of her just like the world had. It left an empty hole of despair that she would fill by helping her friend and the child that she carried. That baby was their hope now and they must cherish it. Taking a breath, she willed herself to speak, for this meeting could see them on the streets and how would she help mother and child then?

"I am sorry, Sir. Please begin. I will do my best to comfort the widow through this procedure. I understand how difficult this must be for you."

The lawyer was a pointy-faced man with large ears, a combination that gave him the air of a satirical drawing of a rat in a top hat. Nodding his agreement, he began:

"This is the last will and testament of me,

William Richmond of Henley-on-Thames, and replaces and supersedes all previous wills and testaments made by myself. First, I will that all my just debts, my legal and funeral expenses be paid by my executor named below. From the remaining body of wealth, I give and bequeath the use and enjoyment only of my properties and lands, all household goods and furniture, and any monies, stocks, shares, bonds, securities for money and all other parts of my present estate and effects what-so-ever and where-so-ever unto my wife, Mrs Nora Richmond, for her entire lifetime of widowhood..."

Valeria let out a breath. That, at least, was a relief. She knew that William's family loathed Nora and if he had not updated his Will to include her, it would have been a dark day indeed. It seemed unlikely that the natural inheritors and inheritrices of his estate under the Queen's law would have been willing to keep Nora and her child housed at their considerable expense.

When he finally finished, the lawyer looked at Nora. With an expression that seemed to find her emotional outburst as being so distasteful he could not bear to speak to her, he turned to Valeria. "For now, Mrs Richmond is in a very good place. However, there are a number of matters to pay attention to here. The first is that you will need to sell some of the estate to pay off a large portion of the inheritance taxes and the considerable loans which are outstanding for equipment bought on credit."

"My understanding is that those creditors do not expect full payment now, they have contracts to be paid down over months or years," Valeria said.

"That was true until Mr Richmond died. Now those creditors are within their rights to collect the debt from you immediately. Invariably in cases like this, they do. There are also other costs, the household staff, my own legal fees, a memorial service... all this costs money and not only were most of Mr Richmond's assets not in an easily liquidated form, but the patents he hoped would bring in an income for himself and Mrs Richmond are not profitable yet. Many of his designs are awaiting the building of appropriate factories. These were long term investments, you see."

Valeria's heart was sinking, this was her remaining fear that had gone unrealised until now. That she, Nora, and the baby would be rendered homeless.

"I do see," Valeria said.

"The other issue is that a large part of Mr Richmond's income still came from his family by way of an annual allowance. We can expect that to dry up now as well, given the family's feelings about Mrs Richmond."

"What are you implying?"

"I do not mean to offend. However, it is known that Mr Richmond's family did not take kindly to his marrying an orphan of no name, no family, and no money. Forgive me, but at this time, it would be inadvisable to allow myself to obscure the truth with manners."

"Very well. Thank you for your candour. What would you recommend that Mrs Richmond do?"

"Well, the family are anxious to buy Mrs Richmond out, they would provide a cash sum in return for all the properties, work and creations of Mr Richmond. That could allow her a new start with the child as a reasonably well-off widow."

"No," Nora whispered. It was the clearest and most decisive thing she had said in days. "It is not Mr Richmond's work. It is our work. My hand is in the research as much as his and it is a part of him I still have. They will not take it away from my baby and me. This is our *home*."

Valeria's heart sank. Nora could either run this place into the ground or eke out a living on a cash settlement that would bring with it no longer-term income but the bank interest. A greasy sick feeling settled in her stomach... there was an alternative, one that might still be open to her, and only her.

It was a horrible prospect, one that felt like she would be accepting a kind of death.

But that was pride talking. It was not death. It was a way of keeping life going. Life for her, for Nora, and above all, for the baby.

"Please, Sir," she said to the lawyer. "Could you hail a cab for me. There may be a solution to Mrs Richmond's financial matters, but I must go now to see about it."

The lawyer nodded. "Do not take too long, your situation here is untenable."

Within the hour Valeria was dismounting from a cab on the edge of town and walking up the long driveway to Miss Umbridge's house.

8

Thomas sat behind the desk and did his best not to crow at Valeria's defeat. Though he could not prevent the smug grin that lit up his face.

That great joy turned Valeria's stomach even further. It hurt to see how great a joy this was to him, how much he felt her loss as a victory. She could see how much it cost him to remain magnanimous but he did and managed to cultivate the odious air that he had expected her to agree in the end. This was not the elations of a lover whose proposal had been accepted, this was the sadistic pleasure of the victor who has slaughtered his enemies and claimed their daughters as his wives.

Valeria sat in silence as he spoke.

"Of course, my dearest Valeria. We will hold the service here, the same priest who presided over Miss Umbridge's wedding shall marry us. That is most appropriate and I'm sure she would approve."

Valeria kept her face blank. She hoped that Delores would not be aware of the awful position she had put her in. In her own way the woman had tried to provide for her. Despite how awful this marriage would be she felt another stab of grief and silently thanked Delores for her care.

"She was the closest thing to a mother to me, so I hope so."

That caused his nose to wrinkle with distaste. "Hers was one of the first marriages he, the priest, presided over. Since then, he buried her husband when he passed, and buried her in her turn. Now he shall marry us in this house. He is old, so it might be one of his last marriages. Would that not be most poetic? What a delightful link with the past."

Valeria said nothing and sat sullenly in the seat in front of Mr Wright's desk. Slowly she nodded.

"I do have to ask, are you a maid?"

Heat flooded her cheeks and anger filled her with its power. How dare he ask such a thing?

"Does it matter?"

The smile fell off his face. "Of course, it matters, you are to be my wife."

Valeria felt that anger inside as hot as a furnace. As hot as the engines that would power the steamship *Catherine the Great* but she had to bite it down. The man wanted the money but men could be prideful and she must find a way to keep Nora safe. This inheritance would allow her to do that.

"You get the inheritance either way... however, yes, I am still a maid."

"Then, will you become my wife?"

Valeria swallowed down the bile that threatened to choke her and delivered her four-word message, "Mr Wright, I accept."

All she wanted to do was leave but she listened to him expanding on his plans for their life together. As he did a quiet calm acceptance came over her. She had survived, day after day, of appalling abuse at the hands of Miss June. She could live under this man's thumb.

"Of course, we shall get you pregnant as soon as possible. I want many children. I cannot bear the idea of leaving this estate outside the family, nor to any of my living relatives. The oldest shall inherit all, of course, with an income for the others derived from his incomes on the land. But we must have as many sons as possible for children die all too often. My sister lost all three of her children to fevers. Though she was a careless wench. She died herself of a fever not long after the third..."

On and on he went.

Valeria held her mouth in a tight rictus of a grin at first, but soon it became clear that he required no reaction from her, no response, either verbal, or in the expression of her face. So, she allowed her false cheer to drop and did not even pretend to listen anymore. Instead, she imagined the life she would be able to provide for Nora and Nora's child in the wake of this wedding.

It would mean shouldering the burden of living with this man. Accepting his kisses, his more intimate advances, perhaps even, yes, bearing his children. But all this was better than Miss June and her orphanage, was better than the poorhouse.

She knew better than to invest her hope the way Nora had. Allen had been a beautiful dream, a wonderful interlude that would keep her warm throughout the long cold years to come. To wish for his return was to make the reality where he was dead too unbearable to live in. She began, for the first time, to understand what Nora meant about the nature of true hopelessness.

Besides, she thought silently as she looked around the library, there are always books to fall back to, or rather into. She could always escape Mr Wright —Thomas as she must now call him. She could always escape Thomas by opening one of these books and becoming Penelope living among the suitors and pining for a drowned husband. Or Medea who fed her own children to their father for his betrayal. Or perhaps Clytemnestra who carved her husband up while he was bathing.

It cost her much to sit there and let him talk the way he was. She wanted with all her being to take back her consent. To save herself from this marriage, but to do so would be to condemn herself and Nora to a long slow slide into poverty.

Marriage and hanging go by destiny, she thought. Matches are made in heaven or in hell.

He looked at her with a smile, and seemed to see her properly for the first time since she had said her four-word acceptance of his damned proposal. She was pleased to see the smug smile on his face fade a little.

"What is wrong, my love?" he asked her, with something approaching genuine concern. "An engagement should be a celebratory affair. Let us drink a toast to our nuptials."

She smiled, and politely declined. His face hardened, as he poured two brandies from a bottle in his desk drawer. "You will do as I say. We are celebrating."

"You are celebrating. My feelings have not changed."

"Then why have you accepted me as your husband? For the money alone?"

She leaned forward and looked him in the eyes. "Yes, for the money alone."

He smiled a smile of triumph and her skin crawled. He did not need the love of his wife only her subservience. She would have been better to pretend to have come around, to have fallen in love. Instead, she had given him the last bargaining chip she had — her dignity.

"You must be in terrible straits to throw your maidenhood and freedom away on me if you still feel as you did when last we spoke on this subject. If I remember correctly you made me feel a fool for thinking a man like me could be loved by a woman like you."

"I said no such—"

"You will shut your mouth when I am talking,

Valeria." He spat the words with such anger and venom that she fell silent. "You made me feel as though I were not worthy of you. You? Who are you to lord it about a house like this? An orphan of no name, of no family, wealth, connections, friends... you can't point to a pet animal that loves you. Yet, you condescend to me. I will marry you, Valeria, but you will learn to respect your betters."

She wanted to respond, but he was livid, so angry he might break the contract with her and that would mean an end for Nora and her child. For them, Valeria could take this, she could take anything. This was nothing to the physical assaults of Miss June.

"Your silence suggests you learn fast. I do not need my wife to love me. I need her to be beautiful, to respect me, and to serve my wishes. Though you say you are... I do not even need you to be pure. Lord knows I've heard stories about how orphanages make their money from their wards. You will do this — be beautiful, respect me, and serve my every wish — because if you do not do exactly as I wish of you, you will go back to whatever predicament you crawled out of and your share of the money evaporates. DO YOU UNDERSTAND ME?"

Valeria bowed her head and nodded.

"Look me in the eye," Mr Wright snarled. "And speak up."

Valeria looked at him, met his fanatical eyes, and said, "I understand."

And she truly did, money would make this easier, but only by so much. The dresses and stately rooms would all be gilding on an iron cage, and this prison guard had the same tone as Miss June. A little person given more power than they are used to, much more power than they deserved.

She did not understand how it was that some people when trodden down could come out like Miss June, or Sophie, or Mr Wright, while others could be as kind as Nora was and Allen had been. Perhaps it was just that there was good and bad everywhere one looked. And in this world, it was the bad that won out time and time again. Allen died and Thomas was to marry her and win a great fortune.

She understood that Miss Umbridge had meant this to be a method of saving her, to wed her to a lawyer with a fine business and settle on them a large inheritance. It was an act of kindness from her saviour. But to her at that moment it felt like spite, unforgiven for bringing Allen into the home. The old woman was reaching up from beyond the grave to punish Valeria again for her perceived crimes.

Valeria wanted to whisper something to Miss Umbridge's ghost, but she knew that haunted as this house was, it was not by those dead and gone. The horrors that stalked the shadow of this house were the prospects of a future lived here as Mrs Valeria Wright, prisoner-wife to this sadistic coward.

She picked up the glass he had poured and drained the brandy from it. The alcohol burned on the way down, scorching her throat and spreading its warm fingers through her stomach. It gave her a little relief.

"I will believe you for now. You are to be my wife, I consider this the maid's blessing, make sure you stay that way until the wedding."

Valeria nodded as she made her way out of the library. Cookie met her in the hall as she left, her face was one of horrified pity.

"Miss Collins, what have you done?" she asked. "You have not let that man have you? You got out of his circle, girl. Why would you let him draw you back in?"

"I had to, Cookie," Valeria said, feeling her courage leaving her. "I have to look after my friends."

Cookie was looking at her with such a look of sadness on her face that she could barely stand to face her. Cookie opened her arms and Valeria fell forward into them. The sturdy servant woman wrapped her arms about Valeria and Valeria felt a rush of reassurance. The flood broke and she buried her face in Cookie's shoulder. The starched cloth of her uniform scratched her face, but softened as it slowly absorbed her tears.

"There, there now, Miss Collins — Valeria, it is quite a sacrifice to take that animal into your marriage bed, but he comes with a good fortune and perhaps you can do some good for the people like me who live under his vicious thumb. It ain't right that the world puts power and money in the hands of men like him, when women like you are given nothing. Perhaps this goes some way to evening that score."

Of course, they both knew it did not. That there was no will in the world that could even that score but the word of the Queen and her Parliament of monied men who made the rules. She felt a deep bitterness then towards the whole pack of them. The lawmakers and the ancient orders that had built the cage that trapped her and Nora from birth. One which kept closing on them, every time an exit seemed to present itself to their harried and beleaguered eyes.

When she finally pulled away from Cook's hug,

she found she left behind a perfect mask in the damp patches her tears had stained into the white of Cook's apron.

"I'm sorry," she said.

"So am I, Miss Valeria," Cookie said.

9

Still feeling sick with grief and sorrow for her own future, Valeria had returned to the house once filled with love. There she had explained to the lawyer and to Nora that the situation was resolved.

The lawyer nodded, seeming way too pleased at the idea. It seemed that marriage to a wealthy man was his idea of her place in the world and he did not care what that man was like. Or what that marriage would cost her poor broken heart.

To Nora she had said very little about Thomas. She didn't need to for her friend already knew what a fiend he was. Now she had tried to make light of the peril this marriage put her in and the hardships it would bring. It didn't work. But Nora and she had been friends since they were so small. They had protected each other at the orphanage and it was only right that they continued to do so now. This time it was her turn to help Nora.

"You cannot do this," Nora said, for once her tears had stopped.

"I have to do this, Nora," Valeria said, as she tried to explain the situation. "It's too good an offer. I would have my own home."

"You have a home with Stephen and me," Nora said, her face filled with anguish as her hands clasped onto her dress.

Nora seemed more horrified by the idea of Valeria marrying Mr Wright than even Cookie, who had been forced to live in his employ and follow his orders day in and day out.

"I thank you for that and for all you have done for me... but how long will you and Stephen have that home?" Valeria asked. "William's family loathe you, they are coming after everything William owned and that means everything you own. When they do I can either watch it happen as Valeria Collins and we can all drown together, you, me, Stephen and — above all — the baby... we can all drown out on the street, starving and begging until the workhouse takes us or someone like Taylor does.

Until your baby is sent somewhere like Miss June's and we are forced to work ourselves to death or to frequent the back rooms of a brothel. I can watch all that happen as Valeria Collins — or I give you, me, Stephen and — above all — the baby a home. I can keep us all warm and fed. I can do that as Mrs Thomas Wright. Miss Valeria Collins will die out there. Mrs Thomas can rescue us all."

"You cannot do this for me, Valeria. You cannot throw yourself away like that. I could not bear to be the cause of you becoming that man's whore."

"His wife, Nora. I would be his wife."

"No. He does not love you. He has bought you. That is all. You'd be at best a concubine, a whore with a permanent tenure. What will he do to you? How badly will he treat you? I will not let you do it for me. Not for anyone. You can't do this, Valeria." Nora was almost in tears, begging Valeria to relinquish her engagement.

Valeria hardened her heart. She wanted so much to say yes and give up. Allowing them all to sink down. But she had to fight for...

"For the baby," Valeria said. "Will you let me do it for the baby."

She stepped closer and placed a hand on the swell of Nora's belly.

Nora froze.

Valeria could see how much she wanted to reject the offer, to save her friend, but a mother's instincts held her silent. She fought and fought and fought, but after a long silence she let out a long, loud exhalation of breath. "Fine, Valeria. You may do this for the baby. But if he goes too far, if he does anything that I deem beyond the limit, I will kill him, and face the noose for it. So, you do not let him. You fight him on every little cruel thing he does, because if you let him go too far with you, to hurt you more than I can stand, I will kill him and you will raise my child as your ward, a widow to that vile monster."

Valeria was moved — and a little terrified — by this speech from her usually mild-mannered and submissive friend. It had always been Valeria who broke the rules, who chased. fought and struggled, while Nora was the one who stoically took it all on the chin and kept going, head down, eyes front.

Valeria could have kissed her then and there, her protectiveness moved her to the core.

"You're my family," Nora said. "As much as William was and the baby is. I will kill for you both, now that William is not here to kill him for us."

"You think he would have duelled Mr Wright?" Valeria asked.

"He was one of the best shots outside of Her Majesties First Rifles," Nora said. "He would have challenged Mr Wright, and Mr Wright would have weaselled out of the duel like the coward he is and would never have returned to so much as look at you."

Valeria could imagine the scene; Mr Thomas Wright in a field with one of his legal partners as a second, arming and priming a pistol. Mr Richmond was on the field too, but in Valeria's daydream he was not there to fight Mr Thomas Wright, he was there as Mrs Thomas Wright's second.

10

The world seemed to have been reduced to just the repeated sounds of the lifeboat. The beating of the oars, which slapped unevenly in the water, the creaking of the row-locks, the grunts of the rowers and their regular cursing, largely in Danish, unless Allen was rowing, in which case there was a steady stream of Anglo-Saxon invective mixed in with the rest of the languages.

William had not even realised the *Catherine the Great* was sinking until Allen had shaken him to sit up. He had been lying in the dark of their room listening to the bone-shuddering detonations of the thunder, and watching the negative shadows — burned into his eyes by the flashes of lightning — moving back and forth as he moved his eyes.

They had turned out the lamp after it had tipped over for the third time. He had simply lain there thinking about how remarkable it was that so small an ape as himself, could lie there in a tub of metal and of wood while nature's almost infinite power unleashed her destructive power many times worse than tons of dynamite all around him, and he could lie there safe from it but for an appalling bout of sea-sickness.

Allen had found him some Danish plum brandy which had at first helped with his feelings of nausea and illness and then later, made them so much worse.

It was in this haze of brandy and sea-sickness that he was dragged out of by Allen. As he rose, he was aware of two things, the first was that the rocking of the boat was greatly reduced.

That's good, he thought. Might let my stomach settle.

But when he sat up there was something else wrong now. Though he was sat up straight he found his stomach was straining to hold him in place. He adjusted himself until that went away and he realised why. The room was at a terrifying cant.

"Look," Allen said, his voice utterly awestruck.

William's eyes followed the pointing finger of Allen to the porthole.

He did not see it at first.

Then there was a roar of thunder and lightning flashed above them. The light was dimmer down here, not the bright white flash, but a greenish glow. And what it lit up made William finally give up and let his stomach empty. The sickly-sweet smell of brandy and vomit filled the room.

The light faded, but the image did not. Within the perfect circle of the porthole, where there should have been rivulets of rain in front of a roiling sea there was perfect calm and a pattern of air bubbles pressed up against the glass.

Their window was well above the Plimsoll line.

The *Catherine the Great* was sinking and they were already below the surface of the waves.

Their exit to the deck was a mad rush that William remembered more for the abject panic that filled him than any real image of the world outside his bubble of fear. There was his heart beating, alongside his breath which raged ragged in his chest. There was the burn in his leg muscles as they ran up flight after flight of stairs. The banging in his ears of the whole ship being assaulted by the wind, waves and currents.

On the deck he could see the extent of the damage. Port side, where the wheel had once been there was a jagged hole torn in the deck which was already disappearing below the peaks of the waves. The mast was still up, but what sails were left were ragged streamers, which seemed like the flag of some Biblical giant flapping over a battle against the defeated humans who scuttled about on their scuttled craft.

Allen pulled him over to the shortest queue for a lifeboat and they watched the incredibly ordered evacuation. The people could barely keep upright against the rocking of the boat and the battering of the wind, but the Danish sailors loaded them into the boats, put a few competent seamen aboard each ship and then lowered it into the water, timing it as best they could so the angle of the *Catherine the Great* did not tip the life raft as it entered the water.

Then they moved to the next one.

It had turned out the queue for their boat was shortest because it was the last to be launched. However, it also meant that they found themselves aboard the ship with the most sailors, a gamble that now that they were clear of the storm and lost in the open ocean, William took as most fortuitous.

They had lost the other lifeboats almost immediately. Every little craft was scattered by wind and waves, and with the pcaks and troughs being as deep as they were, there was very soon no hope of seeing the other boats until the storm moved on or burned itself out.

William had gone to one of the finest boarding schools in England. He had been taught by furious men who believed in *mens sana in corpore sano* — sound mind in a sound body. And they believed with Calvinistic zeal that the way to ensure soundness of body and mind was work and suffering.

The ancient dormitories had no heating, the pipes froze and the boys would wash in whatever water they could pump from the outside wells. They played rugby in snow and sleet. Did algebra and Latin in rooms so cold they could see their own breath. But there had never been a Michaelmas term that could have prepared William Richmond for the cold he felt that night aboard the lifeboat that saved him from the *Catherine the Great*.

When the storm broke and he sat huddled up with the other survivors who were not rowing just then, he was cold... but, miserable as he was, he praised God... for he was alive.

He did not realise until then that he had expected to die. Had even made peace with the idea.

He did not believe in an afterlife, and feared the darkness after death no more than he had feared the darkness before his birth.

But still he was relieved when the dawn came and he was alive. Because it meant he might yet see his Nora again, might meet their baby... but that was a dream, there was still a long way to go to land and safety.

He listened to the creaking of the boat and the swearing of the men, and ate his small ration of hardtack. The biscuit tasted awful, but it could have been caviar and beef Wellington and he would not have appreciated it any more than he did the salty, dry, weevil riddled bread.

He was alive. What else mattered?

Allen came back from where he had been rowing. His face looked worried. "We have a problem," he said to William. "Looks like we're not out of the woods yet."

Christ, William thought. *What now?*

11

The clock in the corridor ticked loudly at night. With all the other sounds of the house reduced to the creaking of floorboards as they shrunk and expanded in the changing temperatures, the clock became a relentless metronome. The heavy pendulum swung back and forth and some mechanism in its bowels let out a clunk with each swing that went from loud during the day to positively industrial at night.

For Valeria, as she lay in the dark listening to the bowels of the clock thundering out the half seconds until her wedding, it was the sound of some hell bound mechanism drawing ever closer to where she lay, immobilised by fear.

During the day, there was business to tend to.

William's lawyer to deal with, or correspondence for William's widow, or William's widow herself — but at night it all fell away and there were no distractions from imagining what life was to be under the roof — and thumb — of Mr Wright.

She could not forget his trio of marital demands, look beautiful, obey, and respect him. That would be hard enough without having the other duties of a wife to deal with. Till death did them part. Those were the words. There would be no going back, no rescue.

She found herself imagining, as she so often did, the return of Allen. He would arrive, like Odysseus, back to Ithaca and like Odysseus, slay the suitors that had hounded his beloved since he left. Though he, unlike Odysseus, would have remained chaste falling into no Circe's bed or being imprisoned by nymphs. She would welcome him back with open arms.

But that was a fantasy, here she was in the reality of ticking clocks counting down to a wedding day looming up ahead all too soon.

She looked at the window; the light behind the curtains told her she had gone through another night without sleeping a wink. She rose and like a dead person, animated by a sorcerer's puppet strings, she dressed, and went to Nora's room to see how she was faring.

It was strange, she thought, how as she lay in bed the world seemed so real, so close and so concrete. Like everything in it could bruise or cut her. But when she rose and went out into that real world, she found it all felt like a dream. It was all so far away and so insubstantial that she felt if she touched it, it might fall apart like a cloud on the wind.

She found herself reading and re-reading sections from the various travel books that she had found in a section of the Richmond's library. The house might be almost entirely devoid of philosophy, art and fiction but these travel accounts were as good an opportunity to escape the confines of her life as any novel. They transported her to places far away, where Mr Wright would never find her, some places that didn't even accept the idea of marriage.

She sought out and found the passage of de Quincey's on the unhappiness of those who lived through the past and read them aloud.

"I had been in youth, and ever since, for occasional amusement, a great reader of Livy, whom I confess that I prefer, both for style and matter, to any other of the Roman historians; and I had often felt as most solemn and appalling sounds, and most emphatically representative of the majesty of the Roman people, the two words so often occurring in Livy—*Consul Romanus*, especially when the consul is introduced in his military character"

Valeria too had read a little Livy, some of it painstakingly translated by herself, though she could barely remember the phrase de Quincey had found so completely compelling.

"I mean to say that the words king, sultan, regent, et cetera, or any other titles of those who embody in their own persons the collective majesty of a great people, had less power over my reverential feelings. I also had, though no great reader of history, made myself minutely and critically familiar with one period of English history — the period of the Parliamentary Civil War, having been attracted by the moral grandeur of some who figured in that day, and by the many interesting memoirs which survive those unquiet times."

What a time for a man like de Quincey to have obsessed over she thought. This was the moment that democracy was truly born, but now some two hundred years later, did democracy really exist? Certainly not as it had in Athens.

Valeria knew that she was depersonalising her own worries, her own sense of the class conflict and struggle, turning her enslavement to Mr Wright — for that was what this marriage seemed to her — into that noble Civil War between those who believed in the power of the King and those who believed in the power of the people.

Or at least, some of the people.

"Both these parts of my lighter reading, having furnished me often with matter of reflection, now furnished me with matter for my dreams."

How she wished she could sleep and dream herself. Though not perhaps in the narcotic style chosen by de Quincy.

"Often I used to see, after painting upon the blank darkness a sort of rehearsal whilst waking, a crowd of ladies, and perhaps a festival and dances. And I heard it said, or I said to myself, 'These are English ladies from unhappy marriages in the times of Charles I. These are the wives and the daughters of those who met in peace, and sat up at the same table, and were allied by marriage or by blood; and yet, after a certain day in August 1642, never smiled upon each other again, nor met but in the field of battle; and at Marston Moor, at Newbury, or at Naseby,'"

Aye, Valeria thought, all history is the account of

the unhappiness of people. And given time, we are all reduced from people to parts in a history.

She wished herself in one of her dreams. One where Allen was alive and returned, but even then, sometimes Allen would arrive too late in her dreams. He would return from the land of the dead to find that his Penelope had succumbed to the suitors, married herself off, and violated the wedding bed he had built. But Allen was no Odysseus, he would not kill Mr Wright, and if he did what good would it do them. They would enjoy just a short time while he waited to be hung.

No, she must accept her fate. Stop imagining her rescue. Besides, it would not matter in a few days' time. She would be married, and then there was no way out but death. Her death, or Thomas'. She could not help but smile at the words of Nora. That she would gladly kill Thomas if he went too far in his cruelty.

How far was that? She hoped she would never find out. Perhaps he would mellow once they married. His goal achieved, the venom milked from him, maybe he would allow her room to live out her life in the library of Miss Umbridge's old house with Nora and baby on hand to keep her company.

Nora was still asleep as was usual and so Valeria

made her way down to the kitchen and put the kettle on the hob to boil. She misjudged it and her wrist touched the hot surface. Her being tired, it took her a moment to realise what was happening and by the time she had it under the kitchen tap there was a nasty blister forming. She stood there with the cold water numbing her wrist until the kettle began to whistle.

The doorbell rang.

Odd, Valeria thought. It was very early for any visitors to come calling. I wonder who it could possibly be.

She took the kettle off the heat and poured its contents out into the teapot, leaving the leaves to steep for a few minutes.

The doorbell rang again.

Why wasn't anyone getting it? Surely Stephen was up by now. That man rose every day at five o'clock in the A.M. without fail.

While she watched the patterns of steam coming out the spout of the kettle, she tried to let her mind go blank.

Again the bell rang.

She sighed. The tea would be fine steeping a little longer. She got up and wandered through the house. No longer did she worry about opening the door to bad news. What worse news could arrive now. She was impervious to the universe's machinations.

The front doorbell rang once more just before she reached it.

"All right, all right," she muttered to herself. "I'll just be a moment. Patience is a virtue."

The bolts were stiff in the cold air and took a little bit of fiddling to get free but then the door opened and in the early morning London dawn stood two ghosts.

They wore loose-fitting woollen jumpers and oilcloth trousers, their hair was longer and uncombed, and their faces were transformed by their beards. But for all the oddity of their disguise the two figures on the doorstep were without doubt the spirits of William Richmond and Valeria's own Allen.

12

"The winds and waves are always on the side of the ablest navigators," William said, a wry smile touching his lips. "We may have been put horribly off course but it was only a matter of time before we could establish where we were and what was going on. When our lifeboat finally made landfall it was in a region that appeared to be wholly uninhabited. Knowing that trade runs up and down the coast we set off inland knowing we must, and within a matter of miles we hit a road linking one coastal town to another."

"What happened? Did you find it?" asked Valeria, still not completely sure any of this was real. She could well be having a full-blown hysterical fit. If she was, she had resolved to enjoy it. What could be more perfect than having even a hallucination of Allen back.

However, he felt real enough, sounded real enough and definitely smelled real enough, the clothes he wore stank of fish. The whole house would soon smell the same.

She had convinced them not to wake Nora right away, lest the shock be too much for her. Instead, she had gone and fetched the pot of tea and come down to hear their story of how the *Catherine the Great* had been blown off course, her engines swamped and mast broken. The storm dragged them well outside the normal shipping lanes and eventually they had abandoned ship boarding a life craft with a dozen Danish sailors.

"No, we could not find the road no matter how far we walked. In fact, we walked almost a full day due east with the sea at our backs and came out on the other side on the sea again. We had not hit the Norwegian coast as I thought but an island off the coast of Norway."

Allen chipped in. "It was no great distance from there to Norway either. That first day alone we saw two ships' stacks spewing smoke just a few miles away from us, one of the other chaps from the boat said he knew where we were by the position of the shipping lane and something about the birds. But we had no way of signalling the passing boats. I felt like the mariner in that poem: 'water, water everywhere, but not a drop to drink.'"

"It was a tough spot. But seemed no great challenge to a scientific mind like mine and a body with the youthful strength of Allen here. We just needed a signalling apparatus or a way to get the lifeboat around the island. We went back across the island the next day, grabbed our oars and put the small sail up. We found the island was far longer than expected and it took us another two full days to round the southernmost point. Then we set up camp, trapped some local birds, fished up some local fish and lit a fire. There was wood on the island so we took some time repairing the boat, then headed back out to sea."

"This was the bit where we came in handy," Allen said. "We had chronometers, and compasses, all sorts of useful instruments in our luggage. And I'm pretty handy with a hammer and awl."

"Then it was fairly straightforward. We sailed until we made landfall. Sailed up the coast until we found a village. Unfortunately, neither us, nor our Danish compatriots knew a word of Norwegian. There is enough similarity between the languages to order food and drink, but beyond that we were stuck. Eventually, a local fisherman took us up the coast to a bigger market town where we found someone who spoke English. From there it was just a matter of convincing them that we were who we claimed to be, despite having no papers, and that we could pay for transport and other necessaries if they would just offer us credit."

"This was why we were out of touch for so long," Allen said. "I hope you have not worried too much."

Valeria burst out laughing at that, a bitter, unattractive laugh, she thought. Worried too much!

"We thought you were dead," Valeria said, angrily.

"Oh, ye of little faith," William said, a little sheepishly.

"You should be ashamed of yourself, laughing like that," Valeria was almost shouting. "We moved on, made plans, we held a memorial service for you, read your will, we grieved and made promises, feared homelessness."

"Made promises?" Allen asked. Valeria could see from his expression how close he was to understanding what had happened in his absence.

Valeria quickly changed the subject; she could not explain to Allen what had happened. That she had pledged herself to a monster, she was not sure he would understand how she could have pledged herself to another man while he suffered at sea. She would explain how it had been for her and Nora, then break the news to him.

"Why didn't you write?"

"It was quite impossible. They didn't give us the credit we asked for. And the only way we could get passage was working our way down the coast to Copenhagen again. Then the embassy there gave us the run-around; for a few days, they housed us but refused to lift a finger until they got permissions from London. In the end we decided it would be faster to ship out with our Danish friends who were crewing a merchant vessel bound for Calais, then Dover. So we hopped aboard and headed down the coast a ways. Once we were in Calais communication with England was a little easier and we were able to get a telegram off to you. It looks like we have arrived before it did though."

Valeria reluctantly accepted this explanation, though her heart still burned with the injustice of the situation. She had compromised herself because she did not know that her Allen was alive and all this time, he had been so close to being able to reach out.

"I should go and wake Nora, I want to ease her

into this news, she has not been well since the news came of your deaths."

William looked a little impatiently at her. "I have waited this long to see my wife again, I can wait a few more minutes if it will go easier on her nerves."

Valeria could tell how much it cost him to continue to be patient. There was so much love in the look he cast upstairs. His eyes lingered to where his beloved lay in their wedding bed breathing deeply and dreaming, maybe even of his return.

13

Valeria went upstairs with a light step and a lighter heart, she was excited to tell Nora the good news, was imagining the look on her friend's face when she heard. It was going to be beautiful, Nora who had been so miserable, so traumatised by all that had happened, would be restored in one instance.

Valeria would have to be careful, she reflected to herself. Nora was frail and the last big shock had nearly killed her and the child. The news would have to be broken as gently as possible to avoid exciting her too much, too fast.

She heard a knocking at the door, and paused. Really, visitors on a day like this. They would have to wait. She carried on upstairs as the doorbell rang.

At Nora's door she gently knocked and opened the door quietly when Nora bid her to enter. She hurried over to the window and opened the curtains. The pale blue morning light streamed in and lit up the room. Dust danced in the beams of light carried downwards by the cool air off the glass of the window.

"Good morning, Nora," Valeria said.

"Is it though?" Nora asked, bitterly.

Valeria laughed, for once she could answer that in the affirmative without irony or stiff upper lip. "It most certainly is, Nora. Something wonderful has happened."

Nora sat up straight in her bed. Her hair fell in beautiful ringlets, the disorder of having been slept on only giving her beauty a naturalness that emphasised it to Valeria. It was perfect, she wanted Nora to look right for her husband's return.

"What is it, Valeria? What are you hiding from me?" Nora asked. "Have you found a way to rid yourself of that wretched Mr Wright."

The question about Mr Wright killed Valeria's good mood for a moment, but she quickly put back on her smile. From downstairs Valeria heard a raised voice, possibly Stephen's and someone responding.

Understandable, she thought. Stephen will be getting the shock of his life if he is awake now.

"No, Nora. Much better than that," Valeria said. "But first you must promise me not to get too excited. You know how your nerves can affect the baby. You must steel yourself not for disaster this time, but for overwhelmingly good news."

Nora was looking at Valeria quizzically, her look seemed to ask if Valeria had gone quite mad.

"I am not mad," she said. "Though you may well think it is the case when I tell you that your William — and my Allen — are alive."

Nora's shoulder's slumped and she looked utterly dejected. Nora's eyes were filled with pity. "Oh, Valeria. I know how hard it is, but—"

Valeria laughed. "No, Nora, it is absolutely undeniably true."

"Hope can make us believe all kinds of foolish things," Nora said. From downstairs there came the sound of shouting, and a loud crash. "What on earth is going on down there?"

Valeria wondered the exact same thing, cocking her head and going to the door. Crashes from downstairs had not boded well for her in the past, though Nora had told her of Allen's arrival via a window. The once pickpocket had been hiding from the coppers when he dived through a window only to find Nora living there. So perhaps things breaking could be said to be an equivocal sign.

"Whatever it is let us go downstairs," Valeria said. "There you can meet your husband again, saved as he has been from the waves."

"Meet him? You mean he is here? This is not some rumour or theory but they are actually here? Why did you not tell me?"

Nora was on her feet and rushing to the door with the speed of a much less pregnant person. Valeria followed her as fast as she could as Nora, her hair loose and her feet bare, barrelled down the stairs and erupted into the living room.

Valeria followed a few moments later and was stopped dead. Nursing a cut lip, Mr Wright was laid out on the Ottoman while Stephen held Allen at bay across the room and William stood in the centre in the smashed rubble of what had been a side table.

"What the hell happened?" Valeria asked.

Allen's head was spinning. He had done his best to mentally prepare but since Valeria had opened the door it was taking every ounce of his will power not to sweep her off her feet and kiss her firmly on the mouth. He knew, however, that this would be highly indecorous and that William would disapprove. Besides, Valeria looked in absolute shock and should be allowed to re-calibrate herself before being forced to deal with this sudden and astonishing turn of events.

When they had arrived in Dover to collect their newly issued identification papers the harbourmaster had taken them aside and explained that they had been declared dead, the insurance companies and next of kin had been notified and a memorial service held.

It absolutely killed him to imagine Valeria mourning him while he was walking about in the clothes he had been equipped with as he and William worked their way back to London. Without identification, they had not been able to draw down any credit from the European banks. So they had worked for their passage until they could wire ahead from Calais and arrange to pick their replacement papers up when they arrived in Dover.

Now Valeria was sat with them and the world was all at rights again.

He hardly listened to William's account of the shipwreck, the time aboard the life raft, the brief stay on the uninhabited island and the relief of making it to the fishing village. He chipped in when he could tear his attention away from drinking in Valeria's face, her delicate hands, the long shining waves of her hair. He felt the manly pull of her body too.

She seemed a little distracted and would often look over at him, her face betrayed some fear. Perhaps she was afraid he no longer felt as he had when he had left, or — God help him — perhaps she was afraid of breaking the news that she herself had changed her feelings towards him.

His heart sank.

When there seemed a good moment, he chipped in a little snippet or so to the story William was telling, and he read on her face perhaps some pleasure at hearing his voice, his account of the tale, but there was still that strange look of regret in her eyes that troubled him.

Eventually, she rose and announced that she would fetch Nora.

"I should go and wake Nora," she said. "I want to ease her into this news, she has not been well since the news came of your deaths."

Allen did not bother to look at William when he said, "I have waited this long to see my wife again, I can wait a few more minutes if it will go easier on her nerves." Even so, he could hear the effort in his voice.

Allen watched Valeria leave, the sway of her feminine hips, then she was gone and there was just the smell of her left in the room. For a moment he panicked believing she would never come back. He wanted to rush up the stairs again, secure her and make sure she was real, that this was not some cruel, hope-filled dream, some delusion of being too long at sea without water.

Instead, there came a knocking at the door.

"I wonder what Stephen will say when he sees us. How awful that they all thought us dead rather than just missing at sea," William said. "I would have liked to have attended my own funeral. I wonder what order of service they went for. Do you suppose my mother would have had anything nice to say about me?"

"From what you have told me of your mother," Allen said, "I would very much doubt that she would, even in death."

"Yes, she's a tough old battle axe. I can hardly wait, sitting down here waiting for Nora is hell. I am stunned by you and Miss Collins decorum," William said with a grin.

"I did not think it appropriate..." Allen replied.

"Really, after all we have been through together, Allen. And you dare not kiss your beloved out of some pathological sense of finishing school manners. When she comes back down, you take her in your arms, and I shall look away, while you kiss her. I give you my honour as a gentleman, you damn fool." He laughed in that friendly way that he had, which made Allen feel more his friend and partner than his business employee or family servant.

He sometimes wondered about this. Valeria would quote at length from various books that made him wonder if he should trust this man, but Valeria, no matter how often she said, "What the bourgeoisie therefore produces, above all, are its own grave-diggers. Its fall and the victory of the proletariat are equally inevitable," never seemed to say it with any great conviction, and — he suspected — was often laughing at herself and her own revolutionary rhetoric.

The doorbell rang.

There was a pause, and he was reminded that perhaps he was to remain servile. He got up to get the door, but William moved first. "Let me, you've seen your beloved, I am still waiting. Perhaps this is our telegram, and telling the boy off for dawdling will give me a distraction while Valeria conjures Nora up."

William got the door and Allen followed slowly.

"You're a little late with the message — Oh," Allen heard William say. There was something odd in the tone of his voice at the end.

Not the delivery boy then, Allen thought.

Being curious, he sidled up to the door and looked through. A good-looking gentleman, extremely well dressed, was eyeing the rather scruffy looking William up and down with contempt on his face.

"I am here to see Miss Collins. Fetch her would you."

Allen almost laughed out loud at the visitor who did not realise that the man he was pouring such contempt on was his host. William clearly found it amusing too and in his best imitation of a Danish sea captain attempting a run at English William replied, "And who is it calling for this Miss Collins?"

The visitor looked awry at William. "Who are you? You're not on Stephen's staff, so what are you doing here?"

William dropped the accent and in a sharper tone said, "Why, I am here at the hospitality of Mrs Richmond. She likes to keep me about."

"Oh, I see," the good-looking visitor looked repelled. "And you take this pregnant widow's hospitality and enjoy it to the full, I suppose. There is no accounting for taste. I understand the widow Richmond was an orphan too, as is my bride-to-be."

"Ah, an affianced man shouldn't be barging into another man's home when only the women folk are home. You will have to call back later, Mr...?"

"My name is none of your damn business. Will you please fetch Miss Collins immediately? She *is* my fiancée."

At this Allen stepped forward, without the slightest pretence of politeness, he snapped, "What the hell did you just say?"

"Christ, and who are—?"

"Enough, Sir, tell me your name this second or I will fling you into the street head first." Allen felt that he meant it, though to do so might be to render him vulnerable to prosecution from this man who appeared to be of a far higher class than he.

Out of sheer shock the man spluttered out that his name was Mr Wright. "I am here to see my fiancée, Miss Collins, regarding our upcoming nuptials and..."

Allen stepped forward fists balled. How dare this man lie like this about Valeria. Whatever this Mr

Wright's reasons for telling such a mistruth it would be the end of him. Allen was ready not just to lay him out but do some real damage.

Mr Richmond caught his shoulder. "Perhaps you could clarify how this came to pass? My friend here was — it would seem until very recently — Miss Collins' escort around the high-society of London."

Mr Wright's face showed utter bafflement at this information. Then complete disbelief.

He still thinks we're two filthy dock workers up from the boat yards bringing a delivery or something, Allen realised.

"I don't know what you two are playing at, but this is not your home, and as the fiancée of one of the ladies whose home it is, I am demanding you leave."

Allen felt William let go of his shoulder and move a little way.

"Firstly, Mr Wright, you may be betrothed — a point we will return to in just a moment — but as the husband of one of the residents of this house, and indeed the owner of the building and — at the Queen's pleasure — I am the owner of the land on which it is built. Given all this, I am going to ask you to explain to me why you believe our Valeria would possibly have agreed to marry you?"

Allen took half a step forward towards this

odious snob, and the man, with all the courage of the entitled, squared himself off against them, adjusting his hold on his walking stick.

This might get a bit messy, thought Allen, stepping forward. The man took a step backwards and knocked over the umbrella stand causing an almighty crash.

"Miss Collins has accepted my proposal because she is very much in love with me, and I can do wonders for her prospects. As for you," Mr Wright said, regaining his balance. He then turned to face William. "The owner of this house died some weeks ago in a shipping accident. You are an imposter, who will leave now or you will face the full consequences of the law."

"You liar," Allen snarled. "Valeria would never love a ponce like you." He stepped forward, in what he hoped was a threatening manner.

"He's not wrong." Valeria's voice cut through the room stopping him dead. Everyone turned to face her. She was staring right at Mr Wright. There was a long pause, then Mr Richmond asked the question they were all wondering.

"Which of them is not wrong? Do you love Mr Wright here, or has Allen — and if I am quite honest, myself — misjudged yourself, him or both of you?"

THE MAID'S BLESSING

Valeria came down the stairs and stood between the three men.

"Allen's right. I only ever agreed to marry you so that I would be able to protect Nora and her child." She pointed up the stairs and Allen turned to look.

William had pelted up the stairs at first sight of Nora and the two were locked in an embrace, exchanging kisses and cooing over their respective transformations. Him from aristocrat into a rough steam trawler-man and her into an even more pregnant woman.

Allen turned back to face Mr Wright who looked like he had been shot through the heart.

"You bitch," the handsome visitor snarled, his face contorting in anger. "We are contracted to marry. We will marry." He raised his stick as if to strike Valeria and all of a sudden Allen's hand was in agony and Mr Wright was lying on the floor cradling a nose from which gushed a regular Niagara of blood.

Allen shook his hand which showed every sign of having been used to hit someone, the knuckles were already swelling and there was plenty of blood on his fist, but no cut.

Mr Wright appeared to have breathed in to catch his breath to curse Allen, and was now choking on his own blood. When he finally caught his breath and tried to rise, Allen seized him by the collar, opened the front door and threw him down the front steps.

With great satisfaction he saw Mr Wright fall straight into a pile of droppings left by the horse of their cab.

He closed the door and turned to Valeria. "We should probably have a discussion about that man."

Valeria nodded, her face a mask of shame and misery. "I am so sorry, Allen. I only agreed to his proposal for Nora. She needed money, the baby needed money. I did it to save them."

"I know," he said. He felt so proud of her, for taking on that debt, for being willing to sacrifice herself for her friend. He saw courage in her actions.

"Can you ever love me again?" Valeria asked.

Allen laughed. That she had seen all this as something shameful was so absurd to him— but his laugh she seemed to misinterpret. Her face fell further and tears began to well in her eyes.

"How can I love you *again*?" he asked. "When I've never once stopped loving you since the day we first met?"

She looked up at him, and ran forward arms spread wide. He seized her in his arms and lifted her off her feet, kissing her hard on the mouth. She melted into his embrace, and he felt nothing but his hands on her back and waist, her lips on his, her warm body pressed against his.

Then he stepped back.

"There is nothing to forgive," he told her. "But if you are still willing to marry—"

She looked for a moment as if she were about to stop him, correct him and his heart sank, then a look of realisation spread over her face, and he could have burst into song.

"Yes, Allen," she said. "Of course. Of course, I will marry you."

From the top of the stairs Allen heard Nora scream with joy, and William say, "I told you, Nora. He finally plucked up the courage to ask her."

But he was hardly paying attention to them. His whole world at that moment was Valeria, the love of his life and, now, his fiancée.

14

Valeria stood before the mirror and smiled at herself. Having been told again and again of the punishments for vanity, and for seduction, by that evil old harridan, Miss June, she had rarely taken as much care about her own appearance as she might have done.

The dress was simple white silk, the veil was short white muslin set in a simple bonnet. She had not wanted too ostentatious a dress but even with the simple gown, she had never felt truly beautiful until this day.

Lightly made up with rouge and the oily red of lipstick, her face seemed hardly her own. It was framed by carefully coiled ringlets which were very much in fashion.

"You look beautiful," Nora said, putting the last pin in the dress. With great effort she lifted her enormously pregnant body to her feet. "Go on, touch it for luck," she said.

Valeria put her hand on Nora's stomach. The child, due any day now, did not kick. That seemed appropriate, that somehow today, after all the three of them had been through, there was to be no struggle.

Allen was waiting in the garden with William, Stephen and the priest. The household staff and a few family friends filled the half dozen rows of seats that had been laid out.

"Read to me a little," Valeria said. "For my nerves, read me the recognition scene, the moment with the bed." She gestured at the copy of Chapman's translation of *The Odyssey* which Cookie had stolen from the library and brought as a wedding gift for Valeria.

Nora began with Penelope's tricky line, "Go Nurse, see addressed a soft bed for him; and the single rest himself affects so. Let it be the bed, that stands within our Bridal Chamber stead, which he himself made: bring it forth from thence and see it furnished with magnificence."

Valeria loved this moment, the returned

Odysseus sees his wife, and she, who has not seen him for twenty years, ten of war, ten of journeying, she is not sure it is truly him. So, she lays a trap.

"This said she," Nora continued. "To test him; and did stir even his established patience; and to her, whom thus he answered: Woman! your words prove my patience strangely: who is it can move my Bed out of his place? It shall oppress Earths greatest under-stander; and unless even God himself come, that can easily grace men in their most skills, it shall hold his place."

It would hold its place, Valeria knew, because Odysseus had built it himself from a tree which grew naturally through the floor of the room. There was no way to move it,

"For, in the fixture of the bed, is shown a masterpiece, a wonder: and 'twas done, by me, and none but me: and thus was wrought; there was an Olive tree, that had his trunk..."

Valeria had imagined a bed like that, built by Allen, one to which he would take her that night. Nora had taken a little money out of the household budget to send Allen and Valeria to Devon for a week to have their honeymoon. She could make do with a cottage bed, so long as she had her Allen with her.

THE MAID'S BLESSING

The clock struck eleven, and it was time to begin the service.

The garden, with its border of trees was in full spring bloom. The oak at the end was ringed by multicoloured daffodils and tulips in the concentric rings that counted out the years they had been blooming. Next to it a cherry tree wept blossoms onto the green grass paving it with colour.

The flowerbeds were an explosion of colour and the air was full of butterflies and bumblebees rushing back and forth. The whole place was alive in the most vibrant and delightful way. The riot of flowers filled the air with their sweet scent as Valeria stepped out into the spring sun.

Alan stood at the end of the garden, wearing his best Sunday suit, with his hair cut and his face shaved baby smooth with a silver straight razor Valeria had bought for him on his return. It had been a joke about his scraggly seaman's beard which had sprouted in his time on the open ocean and working his way home. She had liked it, for the physicality it gave the abstract journey he had been on. Like the mariner's albatross or the golden fleece brought back with him from far abroad.

Valeria knew William had helped him pick out the outfit and had explained the process of measuring up for the tailor, had probably subsidised the costs too. It struck Valeria as odd that from an orphan she had longed for all the safety of being rich, and she had never been more miserable than when she could have married into true, life-changing wealth. Instead, she was to live with Allen, they would have to work daily to make ends meet, but they would own their home, have each other and, above all other considerations, they would be happy.

She stepped down the aisle that had been created between the two clusters of lawn chairs. William took her by the arm and walked her up to where Allen was waiting. He whispered to her under the veil, "You look beautiful, Miss Collins. Allen is a lucky man."

She smiled silently back. If she tried to speak, she knew she would weep for joy.

Together they walked up the aisle towards her future.

The priest stood under a small bower, built around the swing bench at the end of the garden, and smiled patricianly at the gathered congregants of the house just off Baker Street.

Valeria could see now that Allen was smiling ear to ear, so transportedly happy as to look almost imbecilic. Her heart was warmed, and she knew she would do everything in her power to keep him that happy for the rest of their lives together, till death did them part.

She arrived at the front, and stood in front of all the people who mattered to her, with the one who mattered most, and the priest began the ceremony.

It seemed to go on forever, but she loved every moment. It felt like a dream, not one of the strange and haunting apparitions that had dogged her life since the orphanage, but a dream of untouchable light, something pure and unending. She sat in the warm safety of her own happiness and listened to the priest ask Allen...

"Wilt thou have this woman to thy wedded wife, to live together after God's ordinance in the holy estate of Matrimony? Wilt thou love her, comfort her, honour, and keep her, in sickness and in health; and, forsaking all others, keep thee only unto her, so long as ye both shall live?"

The emphatic way in which Allen said "yes", nearly took the priests head off.

Then it was her turn. "Wilt thou have this man to thy wedded husband?"

Of course, she wanted to scream.

"To live together after God's ordinance in the holy estate of Matrimony?"

Yes, forever.

"Wilt thou obey him, and serve him, love, honour, and keep him, in sickness and in health?"

Yes, with all my heart. She thought, it felt almost absurd that anyone could consider otherwise, how could a feeling so strong not be evident to every person present, to every inanimate object, plant, animal, mineral in the world. She felt as if her feelings were not hers but part of the very makeup of the universe.

"And, forsaking all other, keep thee only unto him, so long as ye both shall live?" the priest ended.

"I do," she said, so simply, so quietly, so surely.

The rings were brought forward, by one of Nora's monkeys. The small human like hands clutched the little gold bands tight and in exchange for a small piece of communion bread were passed to the priest who said a prayer over the rings and gave the larger to Valeria.

It sat heavy in her hand. Nora had explained to her that its weight was due to some fundamental arrangement deep within the structure of the metal, made up of unbreakable atomic units that could not — despite the alchemical magic of Valeria's reading — be transformed from or into anything else. Nora had told Valeria that pure gold was expensive because it was rare, and because it would not react, would not tarnish, but it was soft. Their rings were therefore mixed with a small amount of nickel to harden them, to make them last forever. It seemed fitting to her that the symbols of their love were an eternal circle made from two elements un-tarnishable and mixed together to become stronger and last longer.

The priest took Valeria's hand in his, Allen's in the other and put them together.

A shiver ran down her arm like electricity for Allen had taken her hand in his.

"The vow's," the priest said.

Allen turned to her and looked into her eyes. Through the veil she could still see the glint of a tear in the corner of his left eye.

"I, Allen," he said, "take thee, Valeria, to be my wedded Wife..."

She felt dizzy, this was the moment when it became official, binding before the laws of the United Kingdom of England, Scotland and Wales, and in the eyes of Jesus Christ, Lord and Saviour of Mankind... and, of course, the head of his Church: Queen Victoria.

... "to have and to hold from this day forward," Allen continued. "For better and for worse, for richer and for poorer, in sickness and in health, to love and to cherish, till death us do part, according to God's holy ordinance; and there to I plight thee my troth."

Then it was her turn. "I, Valeria, take thee, Allen, to be my wedded Husband, to have and to hold from this day forward, for better for worse, for richer for poorer, in sickness and in health, to love, cherish, and to obey…"

There had been a great deal of friction between herself and the priest on that little word. She had taken the position that this was the pledge of a slave, and why should she, a free woman of legal age, be promising to pass all decision making to her husband.

The priest had wryly suggested that if she was not ready to obey Allen, then perhaps she was not ready for marriage.

The argument had raged on, with Allen tactfully avoiding giving his opinion on the matter, even when consulted directly by the priest.

In the end the priest had said the marriage would only be binding if done correctly and that meant word for word from the book of the Sarum rite.

"Till death us do part," she finished. "According to God's holy ordinance; and thereto I give thee my troth."

Then it was the exchange of rings, with the poetical incantation of: "With this Ring I thee wed, with my body I thee worship, and with all my worldly goods I thee endow: In the name of the Father, and of the Son, and of the Holy Ghost. Amen."

Amen, she thought. The job is done.

"You may kiss the bride," said the priest, and Allen did just that.

As her veil lifted the world swam back into vibrant clarity, losing the sense that it was a dream. Everything intensified, seemed louder, brighter, closer, and that brightness seemed to transfer even to the sense of touch as Allen cupped her cheek and gently kissed her.

He pulled away and smiled and the congregation cheered a little.

She grabbed him and pulled him back into the embrace, kissing him furiously, the passion of their lips seeming to send a fire burning through-out her entire body.

Then the ceremony was concluded and the wedding reception began.

William had all but emptied his considerable wine cellar of every French vintage he could dig up. Food was served heaped up from a vast buffet of cakes, ices, cold meats, cheeses and breads and Stephen, with the first real smile Valeria had ever seen on his face, played fiddle with the string quartet to allow the guests to dance.

The high-born and the low cavorted together until the sun set and night began to chill when everyone moved inside for port and cigars again provided in generous quantities to men and women alike by the host.

After some quiet advice from Nora on what to expect from her wedding night, Valeria was ushered out with Allen, through a hail of rice to a cab which stood ready to whisk them away to the train station.

When they returned it would be to a house of their own. Smaller than the Richmond's but with Allen's new position in William's flourishing business, they would be able to move into a house on the edge of the city out from the smog and bustle where Valeria would be able to raise her own children, no doubt as friends with the Richmond's children.

For the first time since their parents had died, Nora and Valeria would finally have a place in the world that belonged to just them. They had a home and all the hope in the world. This time they both knew that happiness would last. That it would spread down through the generations that were to follow and that they would leave something positive of themselves behind in the love they gave to their children.

IF YOU MISSED ANY BOOKS IN THIS SERIES:
  The Orphan's Courage
  The Orphan's Hope
  The Mother's Secret
  The Maid's Blessing

THE BEGGAR'S DREAM PREVIEW

It was a cold, rainy night in London. Abigail picked up the blackened old poker which leaned like a crooked old man against the small fireplace. Giving the burning embers a prod, she managed to get a bit more life going in the fire. Shuffling a little closer she wondered how long it would last as she tried to soak up the warmth as best she could.

If she closed her eyes, she could almost imagine she was relaxing inside her very own townhouse after a long but rewarding day at her shop. Her blonde hair would be pinned above her head in ringlets that curled around her face. The day had been spent sewing dresses for the most important ladies of London. Perhaps Miles would be by her side, and they would hold hands in front of the fire, lazily enjoying their time together after a lavish meal.

The sound of her father's hacking cough brought her back to reality. Garth Patrick was sat on their only chair with his one leg propped up on an old crate that Abigail had found on the street. He was using it in place of a footstool.

"Are you okay, Father?" Abigail got to her feet and reached up to feel the temperature of his forehead. She brushed away the damp blond locks from his forehead and could see that his brown eyes were bloodshot. He had once told her that her blue eyes matched her mother's. How she wished that she was here now to turn to.

"Oh, I'm fine, my dear, nothing to worry about it," he croaked.

Despite his insistence, it was something to worry about indeed. His forehead was burning and he was sweating through his clothes, yet shivering at the same time. Abigail was in no doubt that it was a fever. She gave him a reproachful look before she moved back to the fire to tend to the pot of broth.

It contained the last of their food, every little scrap from the tiny kitchen at the back of their one-roomed home. Round and round she stirred, but the broth was getting no thicker. With a slight sigh she carefully poured it out into a bowl. Making sure not to spill a drop, she placed it on the table which was made from another crate with a rag placed over it, to try and make it look a little nicer. Her father tried to lean forward so that he could taste some but Abigail could see it took all of his strength to make the slight movement.

"No, Father, just you sit and relax, I'll help you," she said, gently pushing him back so that he was resting against the back of the chair. Slowly, she began to spoon the meager, watery broth into his mouth. With each spoonful she silently prayed that it would at least settle his hunger and allow him to get some of his strength back.

"I'm sorry, Abigail," he said sadly, "for not being able to give you the life you deserve."

Abigail opened her mouth to protest.

He waved a hand at her, cutting off the words that sat heavy in her throat. Then his sad eyes glanced around at their dismal surroundings. They had struggled for as long as Abigail could remember. They had been lucky to get these lodgings in East London. The small room being on the ground floor provided a huge relief to her father who had only the one leg. Their place was small and cramped and the rent was low, but it was still a struggle to get by.

"You know, things were different when your mother was still alive." He leaned his head back in the chair, having finished supping the last of the broth and launched into a story with a faraway look in his eyes and a glimmer of a smile.

"We were young and very much in love. I'll never forget the first time we met. I was dressed in my red uniform, all new and freshly pressed, proudly riding my horse on my way to battle. Your mother was feeding an apple to her own horse over the fence and stroking its nose as I rode by. I called out "are you lost, m'lady?" with a cheeky grin. "She whirled around, her hands on her hips and put me in my place: *'I should think not. You're the stranger around here.'*"

A sigh escaped him and she thought she saw the shine of tears in his eyes.

"In an instant I was smitten, she was a right beauty and with a bit of spark in her too. I apologised, playing humble, and got down from my horse to introduce myself properly. Oh, I can't tell you how she made me feel. Maybe it was going to war but I think she was just special... your mother. I rode away promising to write to her and sure as anything I kept my word. Her letters kept me going during the tough times of war. Giving me hope and something to fight for. I arrived home victorious and we were soon married."

A cough stopped the story for a few moments but Abigail was spellbound and wanted to hear more. "Tell me all about it," she said when the cough subsided.

"Well, sadly, Wendy's family weren't happy about the match, I can tell you. The Dunkley family were gentry you see and your mother was supposed to be married off to a Lord, not a poor soldier. We were too in love to care about what they thought so we eloped and they all but cut her off for it.

"After a while, her parents' disapproval weighed heavy on Wendy and she spoke to them. Eventually, Mrs Dunkley could see that Wendy was happy and that I would do anything for her daughter. They didn't welcome me into the family with open arms but agreed to provide some of Wendy's inheritance so that she could have some semblance of a life fitting for a lady.

"We got set up in a beautiful cottage in the countryside. Pretty flowers decorated the garden, we had fields and a stable for horses and your mother made the whole place a home. And just in time too, for you came along shortly after.

"The spitting image of your mother you were, we

were a happy family for those first five years, until duty called and I was sent away to war once more. Wendy hated it when I had to leave but I was filled with pride and determination to defend my country for my two girls at home. Even so, I ached to be away from you both. It felt like all my wildest dreams had come true." He paused for a moment, deep in thought before his indulgent smile faded slightly, turning into longing and sadness.

"But during one battle I was… struck down, losing my leg and was sent home for good, no longer able to fulfil my duties as a soldier. With some difficulty we got by, Wendy having occasional help from her parents and I eventually managed to secure a bit of work keeping accounts at the local shop.

"Everything looked like it was going to be okay until that terrible day when your mother died in a horse-riding accident. The Dunkleys cut us off completely, raising the rent on the cottage so that we were forced to move. Crippled and carrying what little belongings I could, I took us into the city and found us room and board in a crumbling old Inn. It took me weeks to secure the job with Mr Walter and by that point all our savings were nearly gone."

Abigail didn't need to hear the rest, she knew how the story went, her hollow stomach rumbled loudly as if to remind her. It had been nice to know more about her mother, though. She'd never heard her father speak about the life they used to have before. His words interrupted her thoughts and she turned back to him. Then she could see that it was the light of love that lit his eyes and she prayed that one day she too would feel that light.

"You look more and more like your mother every day," her father said fondly.

Abigail smiled, filled with pride. There was a picture of her mother with her father and Abigail as a baby above the fireplace. Her mother had been very beautiful and her father was lit up with more joy than she'd ever seen on his face. They looked like something out of a fairy tale, so far removed from the life Abigail knew now.

A loud cough interrupted Abigail from her thoughts.

"I think it's time for my medicine," her father wheezed. He was often in poor health, blaming the damp walls, the smoky air and the diseased rats which populated the city.

Abigail jumped up from her spot on the floor in front of the fire and fetched the bottle of medicine from the shelf. With great care, she measured out the foul-smelling liquid into a cup and held it out to her father.

"Thanks, Abigail," he said, pushing himself up with a groan and taking the cup from her with a shaking hand. He gulped it back in one go, his face screwed up in disgust, "It's lovely stuff."

She laughed, relieved that he still had a sense of humour.

"I think that's bedtime, Abi," he said pointedly.

She wasn't sleepy but there was little point trying to stay up with an empty stomach.

She picked up his walking sticks and held them out so that he could get up out of the chair. As he pulled himself up to hop across the small room Abigail was relieved to see that there was a bit of colour in his previously white cheeks. Though, he was a long way off looking healthy, with his bony frame, and the permanent shadows under his eyes.

"I can take the floor this time," he offered but his insistence was half-hearted and she shook her head.

"No, Father, you need your rest or all that medicine will go to waste." She knew how hard he worked, but he got little in return and he was always complaining about how expensive the medicine was.

After he got into their only bed, he said goodnight and closed his eyes. Abigail moved quietly back to the front of the fireplace. The fire was simmering down but it was still nice and warm so she got as cosy as she could with the ragged grey blanket. She was used to the floor though at times she dreamed of feather beds and cotton sheets. These were things she would have one day, but more importantly she would have food.

As she closed her eyes, she daydreamed wistfully about the life her father had narrated, imagining how different things might be if her mother was still alive. It was so far removed from their real lives. One where they had no food to wake up to, her father was sick with a fever and she was all he had.

Tomorrow would be better, she told herself, she would get work in the shop, have enough pennies to bring something home for dinner and they'd make it to the end of the day without rumbling bellies and the enduring ache of despair that came with constant hunger.

Just a few more years working in the dress shop and she'd be qualified to be a top seamstress. Then, when she was old enough, she'd be able to inherit the shop and be in charge of designing the really expensive pretty dresses that the rich ladies wore. She was always in awe of the fitted, flowing gowns she saw them wearing, imagining that one day she could look like a princess too and then she'd sweep Miles off his feet just like her mum did with her father.

Closing her eyes and rolling over, she wriggled around until she was comfortable enough, listening to the soft snoring of her father and the rumbling of her empty stomach. She wished that her daydreams would all come true, that she could have a nice warm bed to sleep in and enough food so that they never went hungry.

Eventually, the shouts from the streets outside and the stomping of footsteps upstairs faded out as Abigail drifted off into sleep. Her dreams were filled with her mother's smiling face. Then her mother was walking away. Each time she turned a corner she was wearing a different dress. They were all so beautiful, embroidered with ribbon. Abigail kept running through the dirt-laden streets but she could never catch up. Panting and with tears running down her face she caught a glance of her own reflection in the window of the grocer. Her face dirty with soot and her stained white dress looking like a ragged old sack.

Her shabby reflection was replaced with the sight of a loaf of bread, displayed proudly in the window. It looked so tasty and she could smell the freshly baked scent wafting out through the open door. It made her mouth water and her stomach growl with desperation. Her hand reached out to grab it but the Baker yelled out and shook his broomstick at her.

"Get out of here, you dirty vagrant."

The words echoed in her mind and she had to sniff back her tears. Soon all was quiet, her father's snores easing into deep breathing as he rolled over onto his side. Abigail curled up in a ball and basked in the subtle glow as the fire finally faded out, leading the way to a soothing dreamless sleep.

Find out what happens to Abigail in The Beggar's Dream FREE with Kindle Unlimited or just 0.99p

THANKS FOR READING

I love sharing my Victorian Romances with you and have several more waiting for my editor to approve. Join my Newsletter by clicking here to find out when my books are available.

I want to thank you so much for reading this book, if you enjoyed it please leave a review on Amazon. It makes such a difference to me and I would be so grateful.

Thank you so much.

Sadie

Previous Books:

The Beggar's Dream

The Orphan's Courage

The Orphan's Hope

VICTORIAN ROMANCE
SADIE HOPE

THE ORPHAN'S HOPE

The Mother's Secret

The Maid's Blessing

ABOUT THE AUTHOR

Sadie Hope was born in Preston, Lancashire, where she worked in a textile factory for many years. Married with two grown children, she would spend her nights writing stories about life in Victorian times. She loved to read all the books of this era and often found herself daydreaming of characters that would pop into her head.

She hopes you enjoy these stories for she has many more to share with you.

Follow Sadie on Facebook

Follow Sadie on Amazon

©Copyright 2019 Sadie Hope
All Rights Reserved

License Notes

This Book is licensed for personal enjoyment only. It may not be resold. Your continued respect for author's rights is appreciated.

This story is a work of fiction any resemblance to people is purely coincidence. All places, names, events, businesses, etc. are used in a fictional manner. All characters are from the imagination of the author.

The end

❦ Created with Vellum

Printed in Great Britain
by Amazon